The Cloud Chamber

Also for young readers by
JOYCE MAYNARD

The Usual Rules

JOYCE MAYNARD

The Cloud Chamber

Simon & Schuster
New York   London   Toronto   Sydney

SIMON & SCHUSTER
An imprint of Simon & Schuster Children's Publishing Division
1230 Avenue of the Americas, New York, NY 10020
Copyright © 2005 by Joyce Maynard
All rights reserved, including the right of reproduction in whole or in part in any form.
SIMON & SCHUSTER is a trademark of Simon & Schuster, Inc.
Also available in an Atheneum Books for Young Readers hardcover edition.
Designed by Yaffa Jaskoll
The text of this book was set in Trade Gothic.
Manufactured in the United States of America
First Simon & Schuster edition November 2006
10 9 8 7 6 5 4 3 2 1
The Library of Congress has cataloged the hardcover edition as follows:
Maynard, Joyce, 1953–
The cloud chamber / Joyce Maynard.—1st ed.
p. cm.
"An Anne Schwartz book."
Summary: In 1966, when his father's attempted suicide causes the ostracism of the family in their small Montana community, fourteen-year-old Nate copes with his sadness and anger by trying to win the school science fair.
ISBN-13: 978-0-689-87152-8 (hc)
ISBN-10: 0-689-87152-X (hc)
[1. Depression, Mental—Fiction. 2. Suicide—Fiction. 3. Fathers—Fiction.
4. Family problems—Fiction. 5. Middle schools—Fiction. 6. Schools—Fiction.
7. Montana—History—20th century—Fiction.] I.Title.
PZ7.M4716CI 2005
[Fic]—dc22   2004018607
ISBN-13: 978-1-4169-2699-3 (pbk)
ISBN-10: 1-4169-2699-2 (pbk)

For Ken

Acknowledgments

Setting this novel in a part of the country that was new and unfamiliar to me required the help of many generous people who grew up on farms and ranches in Montana and the West. In am indebted to Ken and Elizabeth Love, Donna Hildreth, Janie Cardinalli, Larry and Joy Ganault, and Phil and Sandra Shrug for the time and care they gave in helping me to understand what it means to be a rancher (never more difficult that it has been during these last six years of Montana drought). My experiences, talking with ranchers, have left me with the deepest respect and—more than that—admiration for the women, men, and children who spend their lives raising the crops that feed us all. I am grateful for a lovely novel, *Winter Wheat,* by Mildred Walker, first published in 1942, and the rich portrait it provided of life on a Montana ranch.

My understanding of astrophysics and of the workings of cloud chambers was enriched through the patient assistance of Dr. Ellen Zweibel, professor of astronomy and physics at the University of Wisconsin, Madison; John Erikson, of Lawrence Laboratories in Berkeley, California; and Dr. Andrew Foland, professor of physics at Harvard University. For any young person seeking more information on cloud chambers, or for one with an interest in building a cloud chamber, I want to recommend Andy Foland's highly informative and entertaining Web page: http://www.Lns.cornell.edu/~adf4/cloud.html. You'll find everything you need there to build a cloud chamber, and you'll have a much easier time of it than the characters in this novel, I can promise.

ACKNOWLEDGMENTS

I want to thank Anne Mouen Stahl of Rosehill Farm in South Lyon, Michigan, for her assistance concerning the behavior of ponies and horses. Pitching advice for the screwball (a pitch, not a person; and don't try one at home) came by way of my friend Steven Laska, but I offer no guarantees where replicating that one is concerned. Jaime Stathis, Betty Horvath, Lyla Fox, Hannah Rudson, and Bonnie Sklar were my first readers—always the most crucial ones—and I like to think my story was enriched by all of them. Bridgett Johnson, director of the Lewistown Public Library in Lewistown, Montana, provided a native Montanan's eye on my manuscript—invaluable for a writer born and raised in New Hampshire. Particular appreciation goes to Cindy Nixon for the too-seldom-acknowledged contribution of a great copy editor.

A gift in my life has been the counsel, inspiration, and lifelong friendship of the man I call my brother of choice, Graf Mouen. I cannot imagine my days without his voice at the other end of the phone.

I chose to write this novel in part for the opportunity of working with an editor I deeply admire, Anne Schwartz, and though doing so proved to be one of the more demanding experiences of my writing life, it was also among the most rewarding. To Anne, deep thanks, deepest respect.

Finally, this book would never have been written without the courage of Ken Munn and his sister, Jeannine, who were brave enough to revisit their own story so that I could tell this one.

Author's Note

Although I have based this story on the experiences and stories of ranch families in Montana, the town in which it is set—Lonetree—does not actually exist. Like the characters in this novel, Lonetree and Chance's Dairy Farm, and the Chance family itself, are products of my imagination, though it is my belief that the feelings they experience and the kinds of hard times they live through are ones many others have known.

One

EVEN IN THE PITCH DARK, NATE FIGURED HE COULD
walk this particular stretch of gravel road from the two-lane
blacktop to his family's farm, he knew it that well: the barn,
the implement shed, the pond where his sister, Junie, liked
to launch her little homemade boats, and beyond it, the
four hundred acres that made up Chance's Dairy Farm.
Their land—just a small piece, compared to the ranches on
all sides—stretched out almost perfectly flat as far as the
eye could see, except for a single rise, at the far corner,
where a stand of poplar trees marked the spot his father
called the animal burial ground. Off at the farthest end of
the property, the skeleton of a long-abandoned windmill
pierced the otherwise-unbroken sky.

A long time ago, when he was little, Nate and his dad
hiked to the edge of their land together to watch the total
eclipse of the sun. They'd buried a time capsule under the
poplars that day, with a Matchbox car inside, along with the

1

wrapper from the Mounds bar they'd shared, a handful of plastic Indians, and his dad's old baseball cap.

Today, as the school bus made its way along the dirt road that curved around the barn to where his family's house came into view, an unfamiliar sight greeted him. A police cruiser was parked out front, and in the yard stood two officers in uniform. One he recognized as the umpire from last summer's Little League games. The other was the dad of somebody from school, a kid a few years younger than he was—sixth grade, maybe. He was one of those regular-looking dads you sometimes saw, manning the grill at the annual baseball picnic, that Nate used to wish, guiltily, his own father resembled—his father, as everyone knew, being different from the others.

Nate's best friend, Larry, sitting next to him, spotted the cruiser too. "Man oh man," he said. "You think your family got robbed or something?"

"Maybe some convict's on the loose," said a girl named Susan, who was always recounting the plots of TV shows like *Dr. Kildare* and *Perry Mason*. "And they took your mom hostage."

Across the aisle from Nate, his little sister, Junie, looked suddenly anxious. "It's probably nothing, J," he told her. "I bet they're just collecting for some fund-raiser. More than likely, they want Mom to make her lemon bars again."

By the time he stepped off the bus, Nate knew something was wrong. He could see it in the face of his mother, standing outside in her old blue dress and a cardigan, though the February air was cold enough to sting.

"Take your sister in the house, Nathan," she said, her voice tight and low, as he surveyed the snow-covered yard: the officers, the cruiser, and a second cruiser he hadn't noticed before. Over by the barn a third policeman held tightly to the leashes of a couple of bloodhounds, barking like they'd caught the scent of a dead animal. Rufus, their farmhand, would normally be heading out to the barn for the late-afternoon milking right about now, but he had set his bucket down and was talking with rare animation while another officer—number four—wrote in a notebook.

Before Nate could ask what was going on, one of the officers took hold of his shoulder and pushed him toward the house. "Mom—," he started, but she just stood there, motionless, as if she couldn't hear.

He could make out Larry, staring through a window of the bus. Henry, the driver, was just backing up to turn around. Out the back more kids craned to see as they pointed toward the barking dogs.

"Go on inside, son," the officer said again. Only it was too late. Nate had spotted them. Two other officers moved slowly toward the farmhouse, with a third figure, bent over and staggering, supported between the uniformed men. It took a moment to realize who this other person was: Nate's father.

Junie saw too. She started running toward her father,

running as hard as she could, until one of the policemen grabbed hold and held her back.

"This isn't the time to see your dad, honey," he said. "You'd best go inside with your brother."

Nate stared at the figure, slumped between the officers, moving toward them. He recognized the work boots and the old blue jeans, the mop of sandy hair. The part that was new was the blood, pouring down his face, and the terrible, crumpled expression. It looked as if the weight of the whole world were pressing down on his shoulders, as if something had broken inside him that could not be fixed. He must have put his hands to his face at some point, because they were bloody too, and on his work pants were splotches of deep red.

"What's going on?" Nate called out, his voice as choked as if a pair of hands clutched his throat. The officer was holding him by the shoulders.

His mom was there too, putting her arms around him, or trying to. "It's going to be okay," she said, but she didn't sound like she believed it.

"I need to see my dad," Nate yelled, louder this time.

From one of the cruisers, Nate could make out the crackling sound of the dispatcher on the radio and one of the policemen answering in the clipped tone Nate had heard on *Dragnet,* where whatever terrible thing was going on that week on the show was boiled down to a few flat syllables.

"Victim of a gunshot wound over at the Chance farm," the policeman said into the microphone. "Guy's been missing since this morning, but the dogs finally located him, wandering the back forty. From where the bullet entered his head, you'd never think he could've survived."

"I have to see him," Nate yelled. More desperate now.

"Daddy!" It was Junie this time. They were putting her father in the back of an ambulance that had pulled up, and she was wriggling and crying, trying to get free of the police officer's grasp.

"Bullet must've missed his brain," the officer said into the transmitter. "That's the miracle of it. Unclear exactly what happened. The guy isn't making any sense."

For a long minute Nate didn't move. He heard one of the officers, calling again to get the kids in the house; the barking of the bloodhounds; the police car idling out front; Aunt Sal's car pulling onto the gravel drive next to them. He could hear the faint, muffled weeping of Junie—who seemed to have gotten the impression the blood came from the dogs biting their dad. He heard the cows, overdue to be milked, lowing in the barn and Rufus muttering, "See what I mean? Crazy."

From his mother, no sound.

Nate smelled sweat and realized it was his own. He could feel the thick arms of the police officer, wrapping around his waist and lifting him off the ground, as he bucked to free himself.

"Get your hands off me," he yelled. "Just leave me alone."

"Easy, honey." Aunt Sal this time, her cool hand pressing hard on his jacket, like she was easing an ornery bull back into the stall.

"Let go of me! I want my dad."

He flung his whole body down, scrabbling his fingers in the frozen ground. Hands pulled at him—Aunt Sal and two of the policemen. He could see the feet of the dogs as they pawed against the sides of the police van, hear the scratchy sound of the dispatcher on the radio and, quieter, the voice of his father as he was eased into the ambulance. Not words, just a low moaning.

He tried crawling on his belly. He had to get to his dad, but the hands kept him back. The door slammed and the ambulance pulled away.

One of the officers lifted him up. "Easy, kid. You don't need to be seeing this."

"That's my dad inside. I have to see my dad."

"Your dad's in no shape, son. We're bringing him to the hospital. Your mother's coming along to answer some questions. You'd best let the adults take charge and go on in the house."

Nate kept kicking, so hard one of his shoes came off.

He watched the boot sail past the tire swing their father had put up for them and land in a mud-encrusted snowdrift along the gravel.

"Come on now, honey," Aunt Sal was saying. "Let's you and me and Junie go in the house and fix ourselves some hot chocolate."

As he watched the ambulance disappear down the driveway Nate took a last look at the figure in the back—his father. By the time he reached the back door, he was quiet. He even knew to take off his one remaining boot, along with the wet sock, so he wouldn't track mud onto the linoleum.

Two

EVEN JUNIE KNEW THAT THEIR FAMILY'D BEEN HAVING hard times. Poppa—their mom's father—whose adjacent ranch was four times the size of their own small dairy and hay operation, was always criticizing his son-in-law for not being a good enough farmer. But to Nate, it seemed like his dad had just had a bunch of bad luck: milk virus taking five of their best heifers two years back, followed by a drought that wiped out half their feed crop. Then came the new regulations from the dairy association that required them to buy expensive refrigeration equipment if they wanted to keep selling their cream. For as long as Nate could remember, they'd kept the cream jugs chilled in the wooden box his dad had rigged up in the creek that ran behind the barn. Now the county health department said that wasn't good enough, and the Meadow Gold truck, which used to come by once a week to buy their thick, rich Jersey cream, hardly ever stopped at Chance's Farm.

8

Last year their Mercury needed a new radiator, only there was no money to buy one. This year it was the washing machine that gave out. Nate didn't know the particulars, but late at night he'd hear his parents talking in the kitchen, and where once there'd been laughter and his dad's deep bass voice, now it was arguing, and something worse: a sound, from his mother, of disappointment and defeat.

"It's not Dad's fault we're having troubles," Nate told his grandfather the day he'd come by the house a couple of summers back to find Nate's mom bent over the books, crying.

"Where's Carl at this time?" Poppa asked. When his mom explained about taking Junie to the rodeo in town, Poppa had just shaken his head. Poppa never said much, but Nate knew his grandfather disapproved of his dad. It was Poppa who'd given them their land, and in his opinion, his son-in-law hadn't done a very good job with it. Even with the money their mom made teaching piano, they were just barely getting by.

But Dad had said all of that was going to change. Back in the spring he'd borrowed a lot of money from an old friend of Poppa's, Sam Carter, who'd struck it big in cattle. With the cash, he'd bought a new baler and eighty additional acres for haying, and for a while there he had seemed almost happy. The plan was that they'd hay the alfalfa to sell. Dad had never worked so hard as he did on that grain crop—digging the new irrigation ditches, fertilizing and reseeding the alfalfa.

"This is the one that will turn things around for us, Helen," he'd told Nate's mother. Nights when he came in from the field, he'd set a single stalk of alfalfa on the table, so they could study the progress of their crop. "Pretty soon now the kernels will start plumping up," he told them. "And so will my wallet, honey."

If things went well, he said, they could pay Sam Carter back within the year. From then on, it would all be gravy. Nate could get a bike his own size instead of the old red Pee Wee lowrider he'd had since he was seven, and Junie could get a regular horse she could actually ride instead of the crazy pony they had now, and maybe a saddle to boot. They'd fix the suspension on the Mercury station wagon and the four keys on his mother's piano that had stopped sounding, making odd little gaps in the music when she played. Maybe they'd even get a telescope.

"Come harvesttime, even your father will have to say I did something right," Dad told Mom, the two of them standing on the edge of the field one late June evening, watching the sun set over the Crazy Mountains and the hawks circling above their plump and golden crop of grain.

The last week in July that year, a strange, heavy stillness came over the farm. "High pressure area," his father said. "Looks to me like a summer storm brewing. One last good rain—just what we need before harvest."

All day the sky was the flat, dull gray of a battleship, but then it suddenly grew dark as mud. The wind grew still, and a strange, eerie smell seemed to hang over them. Even the cows in the field behind the barn sensed something was coming, milling around like restless schoolchildren during a fire drill. The weather vane didn't rotate even half an inch.

Then it happened: a freak storm, with hailstones big as baseballs pounding down so hard that one dented the Mercury. Theirs was the only place in the whole county that was hit.

Fifteen minutes later it was over, but the damage had been done: Their entire precious crop was pummeled, while just ten acres over, Ben Landry's crop of wheat and barley stood untouched. Dad had stood upright as a pitchfork, surveying the damage. But that night Nate had gotten up and seen him through the doorway, shoulders hunched, filling a glass with whiskey. "We're finished, Helen," he'd said to Nate's mom the next morning. "Sam Carter will end up with the deed to our land. Your father will never let me live this down."

When it was over, they went out to survey the damage—he and Rufus, and even his mom, bending over the stalks and studying them. The buds were knocked off the plants and lying on the ground, mostly. Only bare stems and a few battered leaves were left. There was no choice but to sell what they could for a fraction of what they'd been counting on.

Christmas, there had still been presents under the tree, but just one for each of them. By New Year's, Nate's father was spending most of his days sitting in the big chair in the kitchen, staring out the window.

Seeing him that way, a sinking feeling would come over Nate. Something awful was happening, and nothing he could do would make it stop.

Three

AFTER THE POLICE CRUISERS AND THE AMBULANCE
pulled away, Nate figured Aunt Sal would tell him and Junie
what had happened. But as she set the hot chocolate down
in front of them, she didn't say anything about police cars
or barking dogs or their father and all that blood. "Go watch
TV," she told Junie. "Isn't it time for your favorite show?"

Then Aunt Sal picked up the vacuum cleaner and
plugged it in. She turned the machine on, the roar making
it clear: No point in talking further.

"You go on too, stay with your sister," she said to Nate
over the roar. "I'll put on water for macaroni and cheese."

Junie was curled under her TV blanket with her model horses
when Nate came in. The room was dark, except for the
flickering blue glow of the set. *Cartoon Cavalcade* was over
and *Andy Griffith* was starting, with the familiar whistling
that marked the start of the show. There was the boy, Opie,

walking down a sunny dirt road, a fishing pole resting on his shoulder.

In Mayberry—where Andy Griffith lived with his son, Opie—you had mountains with quarries and caves and moonshine stills hidden away and fishing holes where the fish practically jumped onto your hook. Life looked nice and happy. But the thing Nate loved about his own home, Lonetree, Montana, was the vast open space of nothing but sky overhead, the fields stretched out flat and golden as far as the horizon. On this piece of land, his dad used to tell him, a person could spot every star without a single house or treetop blocking the view. From the safe spot out behind the barn, with the moonlight casting a ghostly silver light on the tractor, the night always seemed magical.

Nate's dad had started taking him to look at the stars when he was younger than Junie, even, telling him the story of how the universe was made and teaching him the constellations. Cassiopeia first, the Big Dipper, Orion the hunter.

"See the proud way he's standing?" His dad had pointed out Orion to Nate. "Look how his legs are spread apart, like a cowboy facing down some cattle rustler. Big and bold."

Nate could remember his dad big and bold like that— up on the barn roof replacing shingles, with his shirt off in the sun, or flying one of the amazing kites he used to make for Junie when their mom thought he should be doing the farm accounts.

Afternoons when the two of them finished their milking in time, he and Nate would play ball out behind the barn. His dad had hung a mattress on the back side of the barn wall, painted with a circle for the strike zone. He'd call out pointers on Nate's curveball and his slider and the pitch that had been his own specialty, the screwball.

Over one long stretch of days last summer, the two of them had worked on that screwball. Nate could still see his dad, standing by the barn in his old blue overalls, as he bent to demonstrate the grip. "You start out like you're throwing a fastball," he had told Nate. "Only when you release the ball, you snap your wrist *in*. That's what makes the ball break. Pitch to a righty, he gets it down and in. The beauty's when you've got yourself a left-handed batter."

All summer—right up to the hailstorm—they'd worked on that screwball. Nate never really got it, but his dad said to keep at it. "It'll come," he said. "One day you'll snap your wrist just right and there it'll be. Your secret weapon. One day, mark my words, you'll be out on the mound, in a tough situation, and it'll be your screwgey that saves your hide. Goofiest pitch there ever was."

This was the dad he was so proud of, the dad who could recite the first 136 digits of the number pi and do the Mexican hat dance in the barn, who could build anything, rattle off any batting average, answer any science question, not to mention throw a perfect screwball. This was the same dad who had shuffled across the yard this afternoon, weeping, with blood pouring down his face.

Sometime later—after Aunt Sal had served them macaroni and cheese on tray tables, to eat in silence—Nate heard Poppa's truck pull onto the gravel drive. He could hear voices in the kitchen that told him Poppa had brought Nate's mother back from wherever it was they'd taken her in the police cruiser. If he listened closely, he could even pick up fragments of their conversation—"hospital," "police station," "gun." But when he walked into the kitchen, the room went quiet.

"Hey there, son," Poppa said as Nate set down his dinner dishes. In the fourteen years of knowing his grandfather, Nate doubted he had ever heard Poppa put more than a dozen words together at a time.

"Your grandfather, Aunt Sal, and I are talking, Nathan," his mom said. "Go do your homework, please." Her face, always thin, seemed in the space of a few hours to have shattered. Deep lines creased her forehead. Her shoulders seemed barely able to hold up her dress, and her red hair hung lank over her face.

Nate closed his eyes and drew in his breath, as if he were at bat with a full count in the ninth inning and the game was tied. Summoning his power.

"I need to know what's going on," he said. "Where'd Dad go? Is he okay?"

Silence. Then, at last, "Your mother's been through a lot today." As Poppa spoke Nate's mother disappeared through the door.

They stood there in the kitchen, Aunt Sal sponging off the counter, Poppa rinsing water over the plates.

"Please," Nate said. "I need to know."

This time it was Aunt Sal who spoke. "Listen, honey. You have to understand that what's happened is real hard for all of us. But it's a grown-up problem." She untied her apron and hung it on the hook by the stove. "Your grandfather and I will stay over tonight, to sort things out. Don't worry. Now go on and tend to your homework."

How am I supposed to concentrate on a bunch of math problems when I don't know what's going on? he wanted to yell.

"Best thing you can do right now is look after yourself and your sister, Nathan," Aunt Sal told him. "Everything's going to be fine."

Four

JUNIE DIDN'T HAVE HER BATH THAT NIGHT. NATE LET her wear her summer baby-doll pj's that their mother had told her were too lightweight for February.

Nate read her a story—*Horton Hatches the Egg.* "What do you think Horton does when he needs to go to the bathroom?" Junie asked. "Who sits on the egg then?"

"He can leave it for a minute," Nate explained, wishing she would just go to sleep.

After he finished the book, she lay back on her pillow, holding on to her favorite horse, Midnight. "Natie," she said in a low, husky whisper, "you think Dad's going to be all right? You think they got the blood off him?"

"I hope so, Junie."

"He's coming back soon, right?"

"Soon. Probably."

"On TV, when someone's hurt bad, they can't walk by

themselves. They have to lie on a stretcher. It was a good sign, right? Him walking."

"Probably so, J."

She lay there braiding Midnight's tail, though she didn't ever get it right. "Remember that time Dad took us to the stampede? And that cowboy fell off the horse and there was blood all over him? Only it turned out he was okay in the end?"

"I remember."

"Remember that time we built the igloo and carried out our sleeping bags and made a fire inside and roasted potatoes in aluminum foil?"

"And you got scared in the night and made Dad take you back to the house."

"I wasn't scared," she said. "I just didn't want Mom to be lonely, all by herself inside."

"Oh."

"You think Dad's lonely without us tonight, Natie? You think he's wondering why we don't come see him?"

"We'll go see him soon," Nate told her. "Tomorrow, I bet."

Back in his own room, small as a closet, Nate could hear the little record player that Junie listened to, to help her get to sleep. She owned only two records—"Surfer Girl" and "Mrs. Brown, You've Got a Lovely Daughter." Tonight it was

"Mrs. Brown" by Herman's Hermits. Junie's high, thin voice sang along, then faded out at last.

Nate lay in the dark, restless. Living on a farm, he had seen accidents and injuries plenty of times before—times when his dad or Rufus or himself had cut his hand on a blade or gotten kicked by a cranky heifer. Once, rough-housing with Larry in the hayloft, he'd fallen through a hole in the floorboards, but the lucky presence of the manure pile had kept him from getting hurt. Another time Junie had broken her arm. But something felt different now. Worse.

The picture came back to him of his dad in his chair in the kitchen, as he'd been all winter, looking out the window. His mother, laying a hand on his shoulder, saying, "Talk to me, Carl. Can't you just talk to me?"

Nate thought about the way he'd treated his father, back in December, when that flyer had come from Sears with pictures of all the new bicycles and his dad had said they couldn't afford one. He thought about the drive to town they'd made the week before for feed and grain, how his father had looked over at him and said, "I know I'm not much good for you and Junie these days. You'd probably be better off without me."

Don't say that, Dad, he should've said. He should've told his dad how much they loved him, how much faith he had that sooner or later his dad would turn things around.

I don't even need a dumb bike, Nate could've said. *I just want you.* Instead of the words that actually came out of his mouth: "You promised."

The way Nate's bed was placed, a person could look out the window without getting up, but to see the sky, you had to open the window and stick your head out. Cold as it was, he did. "The one thing that never changes is the constellations," his dad used to tell him. "If you ever get to feeling shaky, you might try looking up at them, see if that doesn't set things right."

Most times Nate loved the silence of the night—when the tractor lay still and even the cows were quiet, and all you could hear was your own breathing. But there was nothing reassuring or peaceful about the silence tonight. Nate looked out over the field—the expanse of unbroken white snow, illuminated by a sliver of new moon—and tried to imagine his dad out there someplace, the same stars shining down on him, through some window, wherever he might be.

He thought about Junie—the tight fist her hand had made around Midnight's midsection as Nate read to her. He tried to think about a great project for him and Larry to make for the science fair. The baseball tryouts in April. The tree house they wanted to build, as soon as the weather warmed up, if they could just find the right tree. Dumb things, even: a knock-knock joke his sister loved to tell people but never got right, with the punch line, "Orange you glad I didn't say banana?" What Larry had told him today: *"You know that weird girl, Naomi? She likes you."*

But the picture kept coming back, of the barking dogs. The policeman with the notebook. His mother, shivering in her sweater. His dad and the blood.

To quiet his brain, Nate began to run through the digits of pi, like he and his dad used to do together. He had memorized up to 111 digits now. *Picture a good time,* he told himself. *Picture someplace different from here.*

What came to him was the summer before last. He and Larry had spent all of June after school let out riding their bikes up and down the dirt road between their houses, building jumps, having races. Behind the implement shed, they'd built a lean-to clubhouse out of lumber scraps. They'd piled a bunch of old pillows and blankets on the floor, where they'd read Hardy Boys novels from the library on hot afternoons. By mid-July they'd read them all and played enough games of cards and checkers that they were sick of that, too. The days that had once seemed thrillingly long had taken on a sameness. Nate and Larry didn't use the word "bored," but they were starting to feel that way.

They were reading a new library book together—*The Adventures of Huckleberry Finn*—when Nate hit on the idea of building a raft. There was no river to float it down, exactly, but the catchment pond at Larry's ranch was substantial enough to launch a boat on and feel like you were actually going someplace.

Larry's dad had shown them a bunch of old oil drums. "You kids are welcome to these," Mr. Kowalski told them. "Just keep out of trouble."

All one day and most of the next they spent strapping the drums together with heavy rope and twine. Nate made the bowline knots that his dad had taught him, and used wood scraps to make a platform to sit on.

They hadn't bargained on how heavy the raft would be, but one of the great things about Larry was that he never got discouraged. Even when they hit on an obstacle like not being able to budge the raft they'd spent two days building, he'd just grin at the challenge. In the end, they had to borrow Mr. Kowalski's tractor to haul the raft up to the catchment pond. Then they nudged it into the water and held their breath.

The raft bobbed neatly at the water's edge; it even kept afloat when they hopped on board. For a couple of minutes the two of them just stood there on the lashed-together barrels, laughing. Then, with the pole Larry had found in the barn, they pushed off and set sail.

All afternoon they floated their raft. There weren't that many places a person could go on a pond, and within half an hour, they had explored them all. This wasn't the Mississippi River, that much was for sure. Still, when Nate closed his eyes now and thought back to that day when he and Larry had lain, shirtless, on the wooden deck of their oil-drum vessel, drifting on the water, looking up at the sky, the memory of happiness filled his chest. He could see Larry holding out a piece of gum to share, remember the corny jokes they'd told each other, and the two of them singing "Ninety-nine Bottles of Beer on the Wall" all the way down to one.

"Let's raise something really neat on our farms when we grow up," Larry had said. "Like popcorn. Or sassafras trees, and we'll sell the roots to A&W for root beer.

"No more milking for me," he went on, chewing his wad of gum. "Only animal I'm having on my ranch is hogs."

"Hogs! Who wants a pen full of big old muddy hogs?" Nate answered.

"See if you still feel that way when I invite you over for a nice ham dinner, cooked by my beautiful wife, Hayley Mills."

"Well, anyway, I'm going to be an astronaut," Nate told him. "Either that or a ballplayer. Major league, hopefully."

"And I'll come to see you in the World Series," Larry said, making their special handshake. "Friends forever. Sink or swim."

Laughing, he pushed Nate off the edge of the raft then. And cannonballed in after.

Five

USUALLY WHEN NATE CAME DOWN THE STAIRS IN THE morning, his mother was standing at the stove fixing pancakes, wanting to talk about the day ahead. His brown-paper lunch bag would be sitting on the counter with a sandwich, fruit, drink, and homemade dessert packed, next to his sister's *I Dream of Jeannie* lunch box. But today it was Aunt Sal and Poppa sitting there with a box of Cheerios and a pitcher of milk.

"Your mother's under the weather today," Poppa told Nate. "I figured I'd stick around to help Rufus with the milking, see you and your sister off to school." He took out his wallet and handed his grandson two one-dollar bills. "This enough to buy yourselves some lunch?"

"Plenty," Nate told him. "I need to go talk to Mom."

"Listen, honey," Aunt Sal told him. "Your mom had a rough time yesterday. I don't want you to bother her. Just try to put all this business out of your mind for a little while."

Junie came down then. She was wearing a red-and-navy-plaid kilt and a green-and-yellow-striped turtleneck, with a pair of orange tights that had a run. She had put her hair in pigtails, but not very even ones. Her face, as she surveyed the room, looked troubled.

"Where's Mom?"

"I thought I'd make you breakfast today," Aunt Sal told her. "Your mom was so tired, I told her to stay in bed."

"She better not stay tired too long," Junie said. "We're supposed to go shopping for my birthday party invitations after school. She promised."

Listening to his sister's small, hopeful voice, watching his aunt set down the pitcher of syrup on the old familiar oilcloth, and seeing his grandfather turning the pages of the paper as he studied the grain futures, Nate felt like he'd wandered into a room full of aliens. Yesterday they'd seen bloodhounds snapping at his father's heels and his blood dripping on the snow. Wasn't anyone here going to talk about that?

"Maybe your mother will take you to buy your cards another time," Poppa told her, but Junie didn't want to hear it.

"We're going after school," she said firmly.

The three of them sat in silence. Junie studied the cereal box, sounding out words. Nate reached for the orange juice and drank straight from the carton. If his mother had been there, she would have told him not to, but Poppa said nothing.

"Chilly morning," Aunt Sal said, joining them at the table. "I hope you two are dressed warmly enough."

Like getting a cold would be such a tragedy, Nate thought bitterly, gazing at his uneaten cereal. Like that was the worst thing that could happen.

"These Cheerios sure are tasty," his aunt went on, reaching for the box. "I think I may just have to pour myself another bowl."

Nate stared at the tablecloth: plump apples and pears tumbling across a sunny yellow background. A picture came to him suddenly, like a random slide that might have dropped into the projector by mistake, of himself picking up his plate and smashing it on the ground.

He looked at his sister pouring milk over her cereal, one of her model horses arranged beside the bowl as if he were drinking from it. "I'm bringing Buster for show-and-tell," she said.

"Don't you ever get tired of showing your same dumb old horses all the time?" Nate pushed his chair out from the table. "The kids in your class are probably sick to death of them."

Junie didn't cry, but she looked like she might. She set her spoon down and studied her brother's face hard. And for some reason, the sight of her doing that—those off-center pigtails, with the bits of hair coming out the sides—made Nate feel even worse.

"Just because you're worried about Daddy doesn't give you dibs to be so mean," she told him.

Then she picked up her jacket and headed outside to wait for the bus.

Mad as Nate was, he almost wanted to hug her for speaking their father's name.

Nate always knew, even when he was little, that his father was different from other kids' dads. It used to be that was a good thing. Larry's dad had all these rules: The kids had to be in bed, eight on the dot; children should be seen and not heard. The Kowalskis had a schedule for when to get up, when to eat breakfast, what the chores were.

In Nate's family you never knew what might happen. When Dad was in one of his moods, you'd better leave him alone. For a few days at a time he might act like he didn't even see you, and you wondered if he'd come in for dinner, or he'd just sit out in the barn in the dark or spend hours with a shovel, digging irrigation ditches by hand, not even responding when you spoke to him. But when things were good, nobody was more fun, and it seemed like he had some double-voltage power pack strapped on.

One time his dad came into Nate's room in the middle of the night. No time to get dressed, even: There were meteor showers. Nate must have been very small, because he could remember sitting on his dad's shoulders out in the darkness of their yard, looking up at the sky. Now and then a brilliant streak of light flashed for a fraction of a second across the blackness.

"The pictures we're seeing are of things that happened years and years ago," his father had explained. "That's how long it took for the light to reach us."

Nate knew what shooting stars were—meteors, falling through the atmosphere. Millions of years before, one had hit the earth and caused a darkness so profound, it had killed off the dinosaurs.

Larry's father would never have watched a meteor shower in the middle of the night. Or built a teepee and slept in it with his son, cooking their own venison steaks over an open fire. One time, when Nate's class had been studying the early settlers at school, his dad had given him a piece of snuff to put up his nose. "Imagine you're some old native chief, sitting around the fire, and there's this white man, giving you these strange dried leaves that practically knock your war bonnet off," he'd told Nate. "And you've got thousands and thousands of acres of land, and he's got this magic little tin full of snuff. So you figure, what's the problem, giving the white man a little land, so long as he gives you more of what's in the canister. Bingo . . . there went the state of Wyoming."

"I wish my dad would be crazy like yours just once," Larry told him the time Nate came to school with an arrowhead he and his dad had found on a trip to Leopold to get a tractor part. They hadn't made it home till after midnight. "What could I do, Helen?" his father had said, with their dinner long since packed up in Tupperware and put away, and his mother sitting there in her bathrobe with a mad face. "How often does a man get a chance to show his son a genuine Sioux burial ground?"

Other kids Nate knew got things like a puzzle or a paint-by-number set for their birthdays. Last year when Junie was turning six, their dad had come home with a broken-down pony he'd rescued from the glue factory. Junie loved horses, but this one—Junie had named him Bucky—was so skittish from years of abuse that even she couldn't ride him.

"Some birthday present," their mother said whenever the subject of Bucky came up. "Your father."

Most farm kids Nate's age knew how to drive a tractor and a forge loader. But Nate's dad let him take out the truck, too, and not just over the fields, but on back roads with real traffic.

"On our road is one thing," his mother said. "But I don't want to see our son driving on the highway, Carl. You've got to stop encouraging him."

"Best protection for a boy against an accident on the road is plenty of driving experience."

"The best protection is not driving in the first place," she said, ending the conversation.

Sometimes it seemed to Nate that his father inhabited some whole other galaxy, whereas his mother's feet were firmly planted in the soil. That day they'd gathered around the TV to watch John Glenn lift off in *Friendship 7,* his mom had shaken her head. "I can't see spending all that money flying into space," she said, "when there's plenty of work to be done down here on earth."

Even Junie knew better than to try to interest their dad in things like playing Chutes and Ladders or setting up scenes with her model horses. He sat her on his lap on the tractor sometimes when he plowed, and she was always the one he brought to the barn to see a new calf. But most of the time he seemed distracted from the business of the farm, like he was working on a math problem as he cleaned out the stalls or loaded up the hay. Watching him do chores, it sometimes seemed to Nate as if his father were some vagrant wanderer who'd just happened by and picked up a pitchfork, instead of the person in charge of the whole operation.

"Do you think I could ever get a real saddle, Daddy?" Junie had asked one time over dinner. "And riding lessons? Like the girl in *National Velvet?*"

"A girl like you doesn't need any lessons," Dad told her. "You're what's known as a natural. You've got this God-given gift, like your mom's got a gift for the piano and your brother for building things."

"How about you, Dad?" she asked him. "What's your gift?"

"Dreaming," he said. "I have a gift for getting lost in the clouds."

Nate always sat next to Larry on the bus, but this morning his spot was occupied by Bobby Lafferty, younger brother of Rufus. Moving past, Nate shot Larry a questioning look.

"Hey, man," Larry said. Then he opened his copy of the *Odyssey* and appeared to be totally engrossed in the story.

"I thought maybe we could go to the library after school," Nate said from his spot in the aisle. The driver, Henry, had started the bus up, and Nate knew that in a second he'd be yelling for Nate to find a seat.

"I guess I'm tied up today," Larry said. He picked at the tread on his shoe.

"No standing," Henry called out. "That means you, Chance."

"I saved you a seat, Natie," said Junie when he reached the back. That was his sister for you. Even when you were mean to her, she could be mad for only about a minute.

Looking around and finding no other obvious place to go, he lowered himself into the space next to Junie. She was leaning over the seat to get the attention of a girl in her class, Debbie Fredricks.

"It's my birthday in thirty-two days," Junie told her. "I'm inviting you to my party."

Debbie turned around. "I might be busy."

"You don't even know when it is, silly," Junie told her, giggling.

"Well, maybe I can come. I'll have to ask my mom."

"Hey, Marsha," Junie called across the seat. "I'm inviting you to my party soon."

"Woo-woo," said an older girl from in front of them.

"Junie," Nate whispered, "it's not cool to yell out stuff like that on the bus. The people who don't get invited might get their feelings hurt."

Junie looked puzzled. "But I'm inviting everyone."

"Well, anyway, it's just not the kind of thing people do."

"What people?" she said.

The bus had picked up all the ranch kids and was now making its way back toward town. Just on the outskirts they pulled up to the small, dark frame house where the new girl, Naomi, lived. Everyone knew her parents were some kind of missionaries who didn't believe kids should do anything fun, just read the Bible all day. Nate remembered the first time she'd gotten on the bus in the fall, how everyone had stared at her as she walked to the back. At the time he hadn't thought much about it, but now he wished he'd been nicer to her.

"I guess in her church they don't believe in using a comb and brush," a kid named Eddie Peterson said as Naomi passed by the rows, carrying two giant book bags stuffed with papers, her hair a frizzy mass. Several kids laughed.

"Put a plug in it, why don't you?" Naomi said after marching back up the aisle to look Eddie in the eye. Nate had to hand it to that girl. She might be funny-looking, but she was brave.

Eddie made a smirking face, but he didn't say any more, and the group of girls around him who had laughed—Caroline, Jennifer, and Pauline—suddenly grew silent.

When the bus reached the schoolyard and Larry got up from his seat, Nate called out to him, "Wait up, Lar." His friend looked back briefly, and for a moment Nate could see the old familiar look, the start of a grin. But then it changed into a mask of uneasiness and something worse—sympathy.

"Gotta go, man," Larry said. "I'll catch you later."

As Junie headed into the long, low elementary building, Nate made his way up the steps to the junior high. He walked down the hall, where on any other day kids would be calling out *Hey, Nate* and *How's it going?* The halls were crowded, as always, but a kind of invisible air pocket seemed to separate him from the throng of others. All around was the sound of laughter and visiting, discussion of last night's homework and the upcoming baseball tryouts.

"Hey, Pete, I brought my glove," Nate called to the catcher from last year's team.

"Later," the boy said. "Gotta go."

In homeroom Nate slid into his desk and opened his notebook. He leaned across the row to a girl, Sandra, who used to come over to his house every Tuesday to take piano lessons from his mom. "What'd you get for that word problem? Number twenty-four. That was a killer, huh?"

"I don't exactly know. Maybe you should ask somebody else."

He was starting to feel like a character on *The Twilight Zone,* like his face was covered with horrible green mold and everyone knew it but him. "Hey, Patty," he said to the girl next to him, "can you show me how you came up with the answer for twenty-four?"

She made the motion of going through her binder, but he could see her skin turn pink. Before she had a chance to give him her excuse, he let her off the hook. "Never mind," he said.

By fourth period Nate didn't even try talking to anyone anymore. It was like he wasn't there.

At lunch he usually ate with Larry and a bunch of other boys, and afterward they'd shoot baskets for a few minutes or maybe, now that tryouts were coming up, go outside and throw around a baseball. But today he moved his tray silently along the cafeteria aisle, picking up a grilled cheese sandwich, a salad, and a cup of chocolate pudding he realized he wasn't in the mood to touch. He sat by himself at the end of a table. He could feel people looking at him; when he looked back, they turned away.

The memory came to him of Estelle Jonas, who was in his class two years ago. Halfway into sixth grade her father was arrested for having stolen money from the feed store where he worked as cashier. When Estelle came to school the day after he went to jail, it was like she'd come down with a sudden case of leprosy. She'd sat at the end of a table just like this, never taking her eyes off her plate, ignored by everyone—including Nate—until a couple of older girls had approached her.

"So," Emily Watterson had said, reaching for Estelle's heart locket, "where'd you get the money for this, anyway? From the money your dad stole down at the feed store?"

"I babysit my cousins," Estelle told her.

"Yeah, right," said Emily.

Estelle didn't show up at school after that. Nate heard she was being homeschooled, but within a couple of months, the Jonases' house was sold and they'd moved away.

•   •   •

No school day had ever felt as long as this one, but finally it was over. At his locker Nate put on his jacket as quickly as he could and hurried out of the building, his book bag slung hastily over one shoulder. He kept his eyes on the ground, so it was only when he heard the familiar voice call out in surprise that he looked up. He and Larry had collided.

"Sorry," Nate told him, looking down again.

Larry started to walk away. Nate drew his breath in and ran after him. He could feel his heart pounding.

"Lar, you gotta tell me what's going on."

Larry shifted his book bag. His baseball glove was sticking out of the top.

"I feel real bad about your dad, Nate. I know it's not your fault, what happened. But my parents told me I shouldn't hang around you anymore. There's talk about your family. You know how it is."

Nate thought about the Kowalskis. All the years he and Larry had been best friends. Friday nights when he'd slept over and they'd played darts with Mr. Kowalski in the basement game room. Mrs. Kowalski ruffling Nate's hair and saying, every single time he came over, how much he'd grown. The two of them lying in Larry's bunk beds, talking about how they'd hitchhike to Yellowstone National Park and—more recently—discussing which girls in class they thought were the coolest and whether Pauline Calhoun was as pretty as the girl on *The Mod Squad* and what it might be like to kiss her.

Nate looked at Larry hard. "Too bad for you," he said, and the tough, bitter sound of his voice surprised him. "I had the best idea in the world for the science fair project we were going to do."

"I know, this sucks," Larry said. He looked like he just wanted to get out of there.

"Or you do," said Nate, and walked off to the bus, alone.

Six

LAST SUMMER AFTER THE HAILSTORM, WITH THEIR battered hay lying flat in the field, Nate's mother had got on the phone with the hay brokers, looking for a buyer. "It's damaged crop," Poppa had reminded Nate's dad—like they didn't know. "You'll be lucky to get twenty-five cents on the dollar."

They hayed a week later, trying to salvage what they could, as the tall, golden stalks of the Landry ranch, due east, blew in the breeze and, later, as tractors on neighboring ranches made their tidy runs, in what ranchers in the county called their best season in years. Finally, after weeks of calling around long-distance, his mother found a stable owner outside of Seattle who was willing to purchase the hay. Twenty cents on the dollar, but it was better than nothing. Sam Carter was demanding payment on their loan.

Dad rented a larger truck to make the delivery run. More than eight hundred miles to the coast—a sixteen-hour drive across the plains and over not just the Crazy Mountains, but the immense Rockies as well. Lying in bed the night Mom had made the sale, Nate could hear his parents arguing in the kitchen below.

"You're crazy, Carl," his mother said. "He can't come with you. He just started school."

"What could be more educational than a chance to see the world, Helen?"

In the end, she'd let Nate go with his dad.

The day before the big trip, they'd loaded the bales on the truck. Poppa was there too, lending a hand.

"Sorry excuse for hay," Poppa said. "This crop lay out too long in the field. If it was me, I wouldn't buy it."

"It'll work out, you'll see," Dad told Poppa.

"Twenty cents on the dollar. Not what I call working out."

From where Nate stood on the back of the truck loading the bales, he felt a sting.

"Hit the road, Jack," Nate told his father, trying to cheer him up after his grandfather had left.

They set out before sunrise the next morning. Junie was still asleep, but Nate's mother was out front to wave them off. "Just get him home safe and sound," she said. "And no dilly-dallying." She gave his dad a peck on the cheek, and he put an arm around her waist.

In the cab of the truck his father put the heater on, and

in a minute it was toasty. He'd brought a thermos of hot chocolate for Nate and a duffel bag he said held their trip supplies: a bag of licorice and a couple packages of beef jerky; road maps of Montana, Idaho, and Washington State; their baseball gloves; and a gazetteer of the planets. "This is what I call living," he said as they pulled off the dirt road onto the tar. "Just me and my boy, heading out on the road like a couple of tumbling tumbleweeds."

They stopped in town for a bag of doughnuts, still hot, and a cup of coffee for Nate's dad. Then they were rolling. Sometimes his dad would tell an amazing story—something from the *Arabian Nights,* or from the adventures of an explorer named Ernest Shackleton, who took a boatload of men to Antarctica, and then his boat got trapped in a block of ice, so they had to eat their own dogs. Other times an hour would go by where he wouldn't say a word.

"Pick a team," Dad said somewhere outside of White Sulphur Springs. Nate chose the Brooklyn Dodgers, 1953 season.

"Who batted .336?" his father called out.

"Duke Snider."

"How many RBIs for Campanella?"

"142."

"Okay, so now give me Gil Hodges's home run total, multiplied by Pee Wee Reese's batting average. And don't use paper and pencil. You can do it in your head."

"You're nuts," Nate told him. "That's probably a ten-digit number."

"What's life without challenges? Get it right and you've earned yourself a licorice whip."

Soon they were in the foothills of the Rockies. Then the Rockies themselves, jutting up into the clouds, their craggy peaks covered in snow. Nate tried to picture what it would be like to be on one of them—like Ernest Shackleton, carrying a pack, with nothing but rations of dried meat and nuts to keep you going.

They passed a station wagon, Minnesota plates, with a family inside: mother, father, and four kids in the back, suitcases on top. As they drove by they did their special car trick. They each put one arm out the window, making a perfectly synchronized waving motion, like they were one giant bird, with a truck cab for a body.

Sometime in the afternoon they stopped for a bowl of chili at a diner alongside the highway, and one more time just after darkness fell, near the Idaho border. Then they set out on the highway again, the lights of the truck cutting through the dark, hardly another vehicle in sight.

"Funny, isn't it?" his dad said, looking out at the desolate stretch of blacktop, lit by a nearly full moon. "At this very moment our bodies are taking in tiny amounts of cosmic radiation."

Nate didn't have to ask, *What are you talking about?* He knew his father would tell him.

"Tiny particles of alpha, beta, and gamma rays emitted into the atmosphere as a result of radioactive decay," he went on. "We can't see them, but they're here, all around us, all the time."

"We studied radioactivity in science."

"Ah, science class," his dad said with a long sigh. "If you want to know what's what, see things for your own self. Never trust your teachers to tell you the whole story.

"Right here in Idaho, for instance. Experimental nuclear reactor over in Idaho Falls had an accident a few years back. Three men were killed instantly from the radiation. They had to bury them in lead coffins, their bodies were so heavily contaminated. The government put concrete over their graves, just so the relatives could come and visit them without getting radiated themselves. You think they tell us that stuff on the news? Not likely.

"See this watch face?" Dad continued, holding out his wrist. "Radioactive. It's radium-based paint that makes the hands glow in the dark. The factory workers who used to paint the dials would have the habit of licking the tips of their brushes, to keep the bristles together, and darned if they didn't come down with cancer from the stuff."

They drove in silence for a few minutes. Then his father spoke again.

"Imagine if we could actually see it. All that light and energy, swirling around us all the time, shooting through the atmosphere. If they could only channel it, there'd be so much power, nobody would even have to pay their electric bill.

"Imagine if you could blast off to some other galaxy," he said. "Never dig one more irrigation ditch. Never milk one more cow or haul off one more stillborn calf."

Then he was quiet, and Nate went back to looking out the window. He leaned against his father's shoulder, not quite sleeping, just taking in the glory of the night.

It was past eight o'clock when they pulled into the Tidy Town Motel in Spokane. Nate had never been to a motel before, and he was so excited, he found himself wide awake again. There was a little bottle of shampoo in the bathroom and a paper cover on the toilet seat and a machine that, if you put a quarter in, made the bed vibrate. He turned the TV on. *Gunsmoke*.

"Man oh man," he said, stretching out on the bed. "This is the life."

"Sometimes I wish I could just keep driving," his father said.

"Only we'd miss Mom and Junie," Nate said. "And Poppa and Grandma, and Aunt Sal and Uncle Harold, and the farm."

"Still," his father said, "it's a nice dream."

• • •

The next morning they roused themselves early. They were due at a stable a little ways outside Seattle to deliver their hay. Nate's father had explained to him that the stable boarded horses for rich people who rode for pleasure. "Wait till you see the getups these types of riders put on," he said. "Hats, boots, funny-looking pants. Gloves, even."

It made Nate feel special, to think that they were delivering feed to rich people's horses. The stable manager had said to his dad that there'd be a man on hand to help unload the bales. "No need," he'd told the guy. "My son can help me with the job."

They reached Seattle at ten o'clock, a couple hours ahead of schedule.

"So tell me," said his father. "Have you ever seen the Pacific Ocean?"

His dad knew he hadn't, of course.

"Well, then, it's about time we took care of that," said Dad.

They drove right into the city, past the Space Needle and the convention center. All around them, people in ordinary cars looked up with surprise at the truckful of hay moving along through traffic.

Nate and his dad slipped down a steep hill with a row of warehouses and rounded a corner. Then they saw it: a vast expanse of blue, with a couple of ferryboats and oil tankers docked at one end. "There you are, son," Nate's father told him. "On the other side of that you've got yourself Japan."

He pulled the truck to a stop in the parking lot at the ferry landing. "Come on out and breathe the salt air," he said.

The two of them stood there, facing the water—the boats, the outline of an island in the distance, a few sails blowing taut in the wind like his mother's laundry on the clothesline, and beyond, as far as you could see, nothing but blue water and whitecaps.

Before, Nate always thought of their farmland as endless in all directions from their house, acre upon acre. But, from here in Seattle, his life back in Montana suddenly looked as small and narrow as a cow's stall. It came to him how much there was beyond the edges of their farm, beyond Poppa's ranch and the town, how many things a person might do with his life besides milking cows or growing hay or playing baseball. Sailing boats, for instance. Catching fish. Crossing whole oceans, even, to other continents, where at this very moment some boy just his age might be standing with his dad, looking out to sea in the exact opposite direction. He didn't say anything, but for some reason, he could feel tears stinging his eyes.

Nate felt his dad's big hand on his shoulder. "Hey, you've never had fish before, have you?" he said.

"We have fish sticks every Friday," Nate reminded him.

"I mean real fish. Today we're getting you a salmon steak. No two ways about it."

The restaurant was called Barnacle Bill's. The salmon plate cost $5.95, but they ordered two of them anyway. While they were waiting for their meal, Nate wrote a note to Junie on the back of the free postcard he'd picked up by the cash register. Even though they'd be home in a day, he was going to mail it.

"Dad," Nate said when the waiter came with their meal, "is our fish supposed to be pink?"

"Stranger things are true."

Once they were back in the truck, Nate and his father headed to the stable to make their delivery. "Valley View Acres," Dad said, looking over the directions. "I want you to keep your eyes peeled, Nathan, because if I'm right, we're about to see some Arabian horses. The horses they keep at a place like this probably cost more than our whole farm put together."

They'd traveled over mountains, stayed in a motel, eaten real Pacific salmon, seen the ocean. Now they were on their way to take a look at some rich people's horses that'd be eating the very hay he and his father had grown and tended all that spring and summer before it got pelted in the hailstorm. They pulled up to a special electric gate, and when the man there heard who they were, he swung it open for them. A few hours from now the crop would be unloaded in the barn, Arabian horses would be munching away, and his father would be driving out this gate with a wad of cash in his pocket.

The stable manager was there to meet them. Just as his father had predicted, there were Arabians grazing in the corral, and a girl around Nate's age wearing tight black pants and a velvet jacket and hat, sitting upright in a saddle, was working on jumps.

"That's one beauty of a horse you got," his father said to the manager, who had introduced himself as Bo Everson. "I bet my little girl back home could give her a run for her money. She's got natural horse sense."

"You're looking at ten thousand dollars' worth of mare," Bo told them. "Margaret there, she's planning on taking her to the nationals."

"She still needs a saddle to stay on, I see," his father said. Nate knew there was no point telling him to shut up.

"So, let me show you where to unload," Bo told them. "I'll just take a gander at your hay here, to make sure we won't be giving our horses any substandard feed. You can't be too careful these days."

"I told you it wasn't our best quality," his father said. "That's why it's priced so low."

They stood there then, while the man cut the ties on a bale and pulled the flakes apart. A stale, sour odor rose in the air, not the sweet smell Nate remembered from seasons past, and the stems were bare and leafless. He hoped he was the only one who had noticed.

"There's something wrong with your crop here, Mr. Chance," Bo told them. He bent to scoop up a second handful, then brought it to his nose.

Inside his shoes Nate felt as if he were melting.

Mr. Everson looked hard at his father. "This hay is moldy and stemmy," he said. "I can't buy this junk."

Nate watched the color drain from his father's face. A vein in his forehead began to throb.

"You can't do this, Mr. Everson," he said. "My boy and I drove eight hundred miles to bring you this hay. I rented this truck. We stayed in a motel. The price I was giving you hardly paid for my seed."

"Now I see why. I'm sorry."

There was more, but after that Nate stepped away so as not to hear. All he knew was, his father took a swing at Bo Everson and a minute later they were climbing back in the cab of the truck and heading home to Montana.

There was no talk on the ride home. Nate closed his eyes but couldn't sleep. No stop at the Tidy Town.

They were back at their farm by dawn the next morning. When his mother heard what happened, she just shook her head, like she knew it all the time.

Seven

AT HOME AFTER SCHOOL IT WAS LIKE NOTHING HAD happened. Rufus was loading hay in the barn, and a line of laundry hung across the line. Mom was standing at the sink.

"We're going to buy my party invitations today, right?" Junie asked.

"That's the plan," she replied.

Normally, Nate liked drives with his mother. They'd talk about the day, and sometimes she'd turn on the radio, and they'd sing along with the country station, making fake accents like they came from Texas or someplace, with his mom on harmony and him and Junie on the melody.

Today, though, he knew they wouldn't be singing. He wanted to talk, and he had so many questions. Where did the police take Dad? How did he get hurt? Would he be okay?

But something in his mother's manner—her back perfectly straight, hands glued to the wheel—prevented him from saying anything. It was as if she'd posted a sign on her back that said KEEP QUIET. She mentioned a recipe for hermit cookies that Aunt Sal had given her and brought up her old subject of Junie's pony, Bucky, who was costing too much to care for.

"If I had any sense, I'd give that horse away," she said. "He's nothing but trouble."

"Bucky's just getting used to us," Junie told her, same as she always did. "He's going to let me ride him, wait and see."

Forget about Bucky for a minute, Nate wanted to yell. *Tell us about Dad!* He felt like punching something, but he only kicked the back of the seat cushion.

Up front, Junie was talking about a visit her class'd had that day from a dental hygienist, who'd explained about tooth decay and the importance of brushing after every meal. "That's so interesting," their mom said when Junie told her how a cavity starts. Nate got the feeling that's what she'd say if he read off the population statistics for every county in Montana or even all the names in the phone book.

In the parking lot outside the five-and-ten a group of women were standing around somebody's station wagon, talking. A look came over Nate's mom's face that reminded

Nate of how he'd felt, standing on the edge of a high diving board at the Y pool in Billings. Junie reached up and
stroked her mom's hair under the pink wool hat. "You look
so pretty, Mama," she said.

"Tell you what, kids. Maybe I'll just stay out here in the
car and let you two pick out Junie's invitations." She
reached over the seat to hand Nate the money for Junie's
purchase. He could see that her hand was trembling.

Nate and Junie headed toward the store alone. Junie
started skipping and reached for Nate's hand. He pushed
her away.

"Just because I'm helping you buy your invitations
doesn't mean we're making a big deal of this, okay?"

Junie headed straight for the party section. "I'll meet
you over where they have the invitations," he called after
her, then wandered over to the magazines and picked up a
copy of *Mad*. He was just flipping through the pages when
he heard voices on the other side of the aisle. It took only
a few seconds before he realized a couple of women were
talking about his family.

"There was always something strange about him," one
voice was saying.

"Myra's husband works on the police force," the other
one told her. "He was at the hospital when they brought the
poor man in. Talking gibberish is what Bill told her. Blood
all over the place. Hard to say if it was a blessing or a curse,

him surviving a gunshot wound like that. Odds are he'll be a vegetable."

"You have to wonder about what drove him to it," the first one offered. "Sure, they had some hard luck, but so do a lot of people. There had to be trouble in that marriage. A man doesn't shoot himself for no good reason."

From where he stood on the other side of the aisle, Nate stared at the magazine—a drawing of Alfred E. Neuman blowing a bubble. Whatever ideas he'd come up with to explain how his father had been hurt, the words he was hearing now had never occurred to him. He looked around to see if anyone else had heard, but all he saw was shoppers going about their business.

"The shame of it's the children," the first woman was saying. "They're the ones who end up paying the price."

"Of course you're right, Sheila. It's not like they brought this on themselves. But still, I wouldn't want my kids spending time over there. You know what they say: The apple doesn't fall far from the tree."

By the time Nate went to the card section, Junie had narrowed down her selection. It was between an invitation with a circus theme, one with bunnies, and one with pictures of little cupid figures in diapers actually meant for Valentine's Day. There was a stack of pictures of Abraham Lincoln on the display, too, in honor of his birthday.

"Why would they sell pictures of somebody who looks so funny?" Junie said. "Our dad's lots handsomer."

"It's a guy who used to be president a long time ago," Nate explained. "But he got shot."

"If it was you, what would you choose, Nate? It's just so hard to decide, when they're all so cute."

"If it was me, I'd send everyone an old used snot rag."

"I guess the bunnies really are the cutest, though, huh?" Junie said as if she hadn't heard his remark. "Look at their little tails. Like cotton balls."

"Let's get out of here, J," he said. He didn't want to end up in line with those women he'd overheard.

"I just want to be sure I make the right choice. Do you think boys will like the bunny invitations, or would they like the clowns better?"

"It doesn't *matter*, Junie," he said. "The truth is, boys hardly even look at things like party invitations. All they want to know is, will there be ice cream and good favors?"

"Well, anyway, this is going to be the best party ever. You'll see."

"I wouldn't set my hopes all that high," he told her. "It's not the greatest time in the world to have a party."

"Do you have to be the world's biggest party pooper all the time?"

Junie skipped toward the cash register, though her step had a certain forced gaiety about it, like she'd been studying a bunch of old Shirley Temple movies and now was playing the part of a girl who was having a good time. She skipped right past the women who'd been talking about their family and a boy a little younger than Nate, whose Dad was getting him a Cubs hat.

"Did you catch those jugglers on *Ed Sullivan* Sunday?" one of the women said to her friend. "Have you ever seen anything more amazing?"

Nate just stared at the women. What kind of cruel thing was it, anyway, to call a person a vegetable?

At the checkout he saw that the new Topps cards for the '67 season were out. Nate looked around the store. There was a woman behind him, fussing with a baby, and at the next line over, a man asking for a brand of cigarettes. The cashier was busy ringing up Junie's invitations.

He looked at the Topps cards again, only this time he picked up the package. He looked around, studying the faces of the checkout girl, the woman at the film counter. He had a feeling there was probably a really great card in this deck. Roger Maris, maybe, or Whitey Ford. He was due some good luck.

He fingered the cards and checked the cashier one more time, but she was bagging. He hunched his shoulders, to make the sleeve of his jacket hang down over his hand. Suddenly he was someone else, someone he'd never been before, the kind of person who takes things from stores without paying.

He slid the pack of cards inside his sleeve. Simple as that, they were his.

"Know what?" Junie said. "I'm going to start filling these out just as soon as we get home.

"Hurry up, you slowpoke," she called out to him.

"Coming," he said, calm as could be.

Back at home Nate's grandparents were in the kitchen. Pork chops were frying on the stove, potatoes were baking. Junie—who always loved it when there was company, even if it was just Poppa and Grandma—immediately began unwrapping her party invitations to show them. Clowns with balloons in their hands.

Nate's mother set the table, then brought over the food silently. As Poppa said grace Nate pushed the ugly words about his father from his head. Instead, he thought about the cards in his jacket pocket. In his whole life he had never stolen anything before.

"So, son," his grandmother was saying to him, "how's school been treating you?"

Nate looked at the faces at the table, moving their lips. He could almost see his father sitting at the head of the table, wiping a napkin across his mouth and saying, *You know, Helen, a man could die and go to heaven and feel life was complete once he'd had a piece of that pie of yours.*

"School's okay," he answered. "There's a science fair coming up. I've been looking for a good idea for my project."

"You and Larry working on it together, I suppose?" his mother asked. Her voice didn't rise above a flat monotone.

"Maybe not this time. I was thinking I might do this one on my own."

If she had any interest at all, she would have said something then—knowing how it was with him and Larry, how they always did everything together. But all she said was "More potatoes for you, Dad?"

Except for Junie, who wanted to talk about her birthday, nobody said much more. Poppa remarked on a particular cow that didn't seem to be producing like she should. "Sure would be a shame to put that heifer down," he said.

"What difference does it make, Dad?" his mother said in that same flat voice. "It's probably only a matter of time before I have to get rid of all eight of them."

Nate wanted to ask what she meant, but he just chewed his food. Junie burped.

"Say excuse me, Junie," their grandmother told her.

"Excuse me, Junie," his sister said.

Grandma and Poppa had brought a box of chocolates for his mother—her favorite brand, in a gold box. Junie asked if she could have the box when the chocolates were finished.

Everyone picked out a piece, making a neat pile of the

colored foil wrappers in the center of the table. "One thing that ends the day right is a good piece of chocolate," Grandma said.

Mom set to washing the dishes. Nate and his grandmother dried. As the group of them stood around the kitchen, a thought came to Nate: It was as if his father never existed.

After the dishes were done and his grandparents had left, Nate settled himself by the encyclopedias. He wasn't in the mood, but he figured if he flipped through a volume or two, maybe an idea would come to him for his science project. From the kitchen, he could hear his mom and Junie working on the invitations. March 24. A month away. He wondered if his father would be home by then.

Out in the kitchen his sister's voice had lowered to a confidential whisper. "I want to invite this boy named Jonathan," she was saying. "But there's a problem."

"What's that?" her mother asked.

"He's in love with me," she said. "And I like him too, but just as a friend."

"Maybe you should just be honest with Jonathan, honey. Let him know where you stand."

"You should talk," Nate muttered.

Nate remembered a day, a long time ago, when things were going well on the farm. He'd just come in from building a fort with Larry and found his parents sitting next to the woodstove together. His mother's hair was wet, hanging down the way he almost never saw it, and his father was brushing the long red curls. Nate remembered his mother blushing—jumping up from where she'd been sitting on his dad's lap.

"What's to be embarrassed about, Helen?" Dad had said to her. "You think our son shouldn't know his parents are crazy about each other?"

"Well, that's for sure," she'd said, and kissed him.

The first two volumes of the encyclopedia had failed to yield any ideas for a science project, and Nate was tired, so he climbed the steps to his room. With the door safely closed, he took the Topps cards out from his pocket, slit the wrapper, peeled back the plastic wrap. No Roger Maris card after all—just a bunch of rookies he'd mostly never heard of. He studied their faces, grinning up at him. A year from now, two thirds of these guys wouldn't even be in the majors anymore. They'd be back in the minor league or selling hardware in some place like North Dakota or Missouri. Or shoveling manure, like Rufus.

That's how it went: A person could think everything was so great for a while there, but odds were high that he'd have a big surprise coming to him. Look at Junie, planning this great circus-theme birthday party. Did she actually think a bunch of kids were going to come to their house, when evidently the whole town thought their family was a bunch of wackos? "Apple doesn't fall far from the tree," that woman had said.

Nate took out a book his father had given him, *The Miracle of the Night Sky,* and opened it to the chapter titled "Black Holes and Quasars."

The gravitational pull within a black hole is so dense that nothing, not even light, can escape it, he read. *Physicists consider that the contents of a black hole have left the universe.*

He thought of his father as he must have been before the police found him—wandering over the back forty somewhere—or over near the Landrys' place, talking to himself as blood dripped onto the snow. He thought about their road trip last fall—the two of them lumbering along a highway in Idaho, his dad in his coveralls, talking about how he would have loved to be one of the Gemini astronauts.

He tried again to concentrate on the words he was reading. *The event horizon is a spherical surface that defines the black hole. Once a body of matter enters into a black hole, it can never emerge.*

"I'll find you," he said into the dark of his room. He wanted to believe that his father heard him.

Eight

THE NEXT MORNING WHEN NATE GOT ON THE BUS,
he didn't look for a seat beside Larry. Today Larry was sitting next to a boy named Travis, one of those fake-type kids
who tell the teacher she's looking nice today, then make
cartoons about her where she's fat and covered with warts.
Nate kept close to Junie, his head down and an arm on her
shoulder, as he passed the two of them.

He lowered himself firmly into the seat, staring straight
ahead, before opening his book. If people were looking at
him, he wasn't going to notice.

For Junie, it was different. She bounced in her seat like
always, calling out to one or two of the kids in her class.
There was a bunch of invitations stuffed into her book bag,
with a clown sticker on the envelope of each.

First period was science. The class went over the answers
to the quiz the day before on photosynthesis first. Then

Mrs. Unger told them to put their books away.

"People," she said, "we have only eight weeks to the science fair. That doesn't give you a lot of time to get busy with your projects. I know you've had your thinking caps on. This morning, as I have told you, I want to hear what you've got planned."

Any other time Nate would feel bad that he didn't have his proposal ready.

"Yes, Jeannine?" the teacher said. "Do you want to share your project with us?"

Jeannine Penney, the star science student since first grade, explained that she'd be pursuing a project in her particular field of interest, human psychology. "I was thinking of using these kids I babysit for as subjects. I'd show them scary TV shows and compare how shook up they were with how they felt after watching Mr. Rogers."

"That's a good thought, Jeannine," said Mrs. Unger. "Just be careful you don't actually traumatize these children with inappropriate images."

"Of course, Mrs. Unger. I'll work on that."

Kirk, known to be a wise guy, said he was planning to study the effects of alcohol. He'd drink one of his dad's beers—purely for scientific purposes—and then try driving his dirt bike through an obstacle course. He'd follow that up with a succession of additional drinks and monitor the effects on his bike-riding ability.

"Inappropriate, Kirk," said Mrs. Unger. "Perhaps if you wish to study the effects of alcohol, you can experiment with the fruit fly population."

There were more: Someone was growing beans in different soils, as expected, and someone else was building a volcano. Sooner or later, Nate figured, Mrs. Unger would ask him what he had planned.

The teacher called on Naomi next.

"This one ought to be good," someone whispered. It was Pauline Calhoun, the girl Larry had a crush on. She jangled her charm bracelet, then flicked her hair over her shoulder and shook it out like some girl on a shampoo commercial.

Nate studied Naomi's face to see if she had heard. If she had, she wasn't letting on. She appeared to be giving all her concentration to a pen-and-ink drawing of some kind of imaginary animal on the front of her science notebook. So much concentration, in fact, that she hadn't noticed that she'd smeared black ink on her cheek.

"I need a little more time to come up with an idea, Mrs. Unger," she said. "I didn't get home till late yesterday."

There was tittering around the room. Everyone knew where Naomi had been: Bible study. She always missed everything for Bible study. She even missed their field trip to the amusement park when her dad made her go to a prayer retreat. In gym, when they did the unit on square dancing, she'd had to sit on the sidelines because her parents thought dancing was a sin.

"I don't have much patience with excuses at this point, Naomi," the teacher said. "You knew for some time that today was the deadline. I'll need to speak with you after class."

Then it was Nate's turn. "I don't have a proposal written out yet either," he told Mrs. Unger. "I didn't get around to it."

"Maybe he was at Bible study too," a voice muttered from the back row. "Or was it visiting hours at the loony bin?"

"That's enough, Eddie," Mrs. Unger said. "I can handle this problem without your participation, thank you very much.

"Since you and Naomi have not seen fit to plan properly, Nathan," she went on, "I will make plans for the two of you. You can work together on your science fair project. I'll expect a proposal by Thursday."

Just last week Nate knew that Larry would have shot him a sympathetic look. But Larry was explaining his own project to the teacher now, something to do with robots. He and Travis had made arrangements to be partners—a team.

Nate looked at his friend. He thought about all the times they'd slept over at each other's houses, the secret language they made up in third grade, the Soap Box Derby car they'd built for the fourth of July, their Paul Bunyan project (him dressed as Paul; Larry, in blue pajamas, as Babe, with blue food coloring on his face that took a week to wear off).

Now Larry was leaning over to confer on something with Travis, grinning in that way he had that always made Nate feel like grinning too. Suddenly Nate felt like Ernest Shackleton, alone in the middle of Antarctica with nothing around him but whiteout conditions in all directions. Worse than alone, actually. He was stuck in Antarctica with the most unpopular loser of a girl in the whole school.

If his dad were around, he would have loved helping Nate come up with his project idea. If his dad were around, the two of them would probably have been checking books out of the library, talking about their hypothesis. He'd be helping sketch diagrams, driving over to the hardware store to get the materials with his son. In Nate's whole life he could never remember a time he'd embarked on a single project before first talking it out with his dad. Without him, the whole thing seemed impossible.

At lunch Nate sat alone again. Just once, he looked over at the table where Larry and a bunch of his other old friends—Tom and Travis and Pete—were trading sandwiches, laughing about something or other. For a second there, he thought he saw Larry look back at him, with an expression that could have been regret.

Nate knew he'd have to talk to Naomi, of course, now that they were forced into being partners. He just wasn't in any rush. Only there she was, standing over his table, holding tight to her tray, with an orange rolling around on it. "Okay if I sit down?" she asked.

"It's a free country."

"So it looks like we're going to be partners on the science project, huh?" She tried to steady her tray while she pulled a chair out.

"Seems that way." He was making a point of studying his milk carton. How was a person ever going to be any good at constructing a science fair project when she couldn't even figure out that a round object on a flat cafeteria tray was likely to roll onto the floor? Which it did.

Naomi got down on her hands and knees to retrieve her orange. One table over, Pauline Calhoun and a bunch of her cheerleader friends giggled.

"So maybe we should talk about ideas," she said, finally seating herself across from him and fumbling to fix the garter on her stocking. "I was thinking we could get together at the library or something after school."

"I'm busy after school."

She wasn't giving up. "The thing is, I guess we're supposed to have our proposal ready real soon. I get the feeling we might be in big trouble if we don't."

Big trouble. Like not getting your science fair proposal in on time was trouble. He knew what real trouble was, and from the looks of things, Naomi probably did too.

"I just don't want to get some really bad grade," she said. "My dad gives me a hard enough time as it is."

Whatever her story was, Nate didn't feel like asking. He wished she'd just leave him alone. Already, he could tell, kids were looking at the two of them. Next thing you knew, they'd be saying she was his girlfriend.

As Naomi peeled her orange he could see that she must bite her fingernails. The skin around the tips of her fingers was red, and the nails were really short.

"I know you don't want to work with me," she told him. "And you probably think I'm a jerk. But you might be surprised. I could end up being a better partner than you think."

That stopped him. When a person put themselves on the line like that, he figured they had a right to an answer.

"It's not your fault," he said to her. "I wanted to do this by myself, is all."

Nate studied Naomi's face, not square in the eye, but glancing, so it wouldn't be obvious. If it weren't for her glasses and that crazy hair, she wouldn't be totally bad-looking.

The thing was, she had this expression. The girls everyone thought were so cool, like Pauline, mostly looked bored. That was how people did it, if they were cool. Whereas with Naomi, she just seemed so eager all the time.

"So what do you want to do?" she asked him. "I

could come over to your house after school. We could talk about it."

"I don't know," Nate said, but she was already working out the plan.

"It's probably better at your house than mine," she told him. "Things are kind of difficult at my house."

Like they weren't at his.

Nine

IN THE END, NATE MET NAOMI AT THE LIBRARY. HE brought along a stack of old *Scientific American* magazines that he and his father used to pore over in the barn when they were supposed to be tending the cows. Their favorite feature was the column called "Amateur Scientist," which included experiments readers might try at home.

"I'd forgotten about this one," Nate said, flipping through the pages of one well-worn issue. "Here's something my dad and I always meant to build someday."

"Tell me," Naomi said.

"Back in 1912 in Austria this guy named Victor Hess started sending up balloons to measure the levels of radioactive ions from rock and water at higher elevations," Nate explained. "But instead of finding what he was expecting—namely, that the higher up the balloons went, the less radiation there'd be—the opposite turned out to be true. So Hess formed a theory that some kind of radiation was entering our atmosphere not just from the earth, but from some unknown source in outer space. Then a few years later a guy named Millikan came along and conducted experiments that proved there was some extraterrestrial source of radiation. He called it cosmic rays. Turns out they're around us all the time. Millions of them. The only problem is, you can't see them."

"So what's our project?" Naomi said, twisting her hair. Nate had seen her do that when she was drawing sometimes, in study hall, and figured it meant she was concentrating hard.

"Okay," he said. "There was this physicist named Wilson who got the idea of building some kind of apparatus that would make it so we could see these cosmic rays, and other actual atomic particles, with the human eye. He constructed this sealed chamber to contain a supersaturated atmosphere of air and water, or alcohol vapor. The idea was that the vapor would condense in the form of tiny visible droplets. If there really were charged ions passing through the atmosphere of the chamber, like he thought, the droplets would attach themselves to the ions. The cloud chamber would make radiation visible. Inside the supersaturated container you'd be able to see the paths the ions made, like a vapor trail."

"And it worked?"

Nate was studying one of the books they had open on

the table. "In 1927, Wilson won the Nobel Prize for inventing the cloud chamber," he said. "And I bet we could build one here."

Naomi didn't say, *What's the big deal?* but he knew that she didn't fully get the significance, either—that seeing cosmic rays was not the same as seeing something like steam from a tea kettle or hailstones on a hay field.

"The thing that's so amazing," he said, "is knowing where the rays have come from."

"And where is that?"

"The far reaches of the universe. Light-years away."

Naomi was quiet.

"The first time me and my dad read about this project, I was only nine or ten, and he said it was too tricky," Nate went on. "But now I think we can handle it."

Not that Naomi was likely to be much help. Still, if they could pull it off, Nate thought, it would be pretty cool. The others would be standing around with their dumb papier-mâché volcanoes and scraggly bean plants—Larry and Pauline and Kirk and Travis and Linda and the rest of them—and there they'd be with this box full of actual, visible radioactive ions.

Bent over the table in the reference room, Nate drew Naomi a diagram of the box they'd need to construct. It would have four glass walls, tightly sealed—like an aquarium, basically, but not as high on the sides—to keep the vapors from getting spread out. They'd set the box on top of a piece of dry ice.

A CLOUD CHAMBER

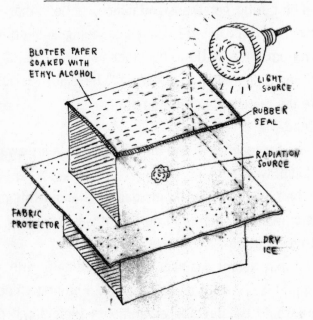

BLOTTER PAPER
SOAKED WITH
ETHYL ALCOHOL

LIGHT
SOURCE

RUBBER
SEAL

RADIATION
SOURCE

FABRIC
PROTECTOR

DRY
ICE

There'd need to be a piece of some absorbent material lining the top of the chamber—felt or blotting paper—soaked with ethyl alcohol, which, when chilled by the dry ice, would create a swirling, cloudlike mist inside the box. Then they'd shine a strong beam of light into the cloud chamber and watch for the rays to show up. If they were lucky, they might even get a photograph, like the one in the magazine.

For control purposes, it was a good idea to test out the cloud chamber first by putting something inside that you knew, for a fact, would give off actual radiation. That way, you'd know if the cloud chamber worked. In the *Scientific American* article, they'd used the face from an old watch with uranium-based paint, just like his dad had talked about.

"Once we know from our test with the watch that conditions are right," Nate told Naomi, "then we try to spot the other type of rays."

"I don't know if I get it yet," she said. "I mean, the difference between what comes from the watch and these other rays. What is it we'd actually be seeing in this chamber that makes it such a big deal?"

"What you'd see," he said, and his voice took on a hushed intensity, "are tiny energy particles from actual explosions that took place millions of years ago. Actual evidence of solar activity. Supernovae."

"So what we'd see is kind of like fallout from space? Like if a car wreck happened, and a piece of someone's windshield that shattered ended up in my yard?"

"Only the car wreck happened a few million years ago, and the windshield's only just now reaching you. Let's say a couple of galaxies collided, back in dinosaur times—or before the dinosaurs, even. What we're talking about is a catastrophe. Something bigger than the worst disaster we

could imagine happening on earth. Imagine the most vio-
lent event you could dream of. Something like that.
Imagine all the energy that's swirling around us, crashing
into the atoms of our own bodies at this very moment," he
said.

"Like there's all this stuff going on around us, all the
time, that nobody can see," Naomi added. "It's like if you
got to put on one of those special pairs of glasses they sell
at the back of comic books that let you see the bones in
your own hand or something. Only those are fake. What
we're doing is real."

Hearing Naomi talk about the two of them as a "we"
sounded strange to Nate, but there you had it. Like it or not,
they were partners.

She looked at him more soberly then, with something
like real respect. "How do you know all this stuff, anyway?"

"My dad. My dad was always talking about stuff like
this. He knew everything there is to know about space." It
startled him to hear his own voice speak of his father as he
did just then. As if he were dead.

"My dad and I are always planning out neat projects to
do," he said, changing it back.

Naomi was quiet for a long moment. "I heard what happened," she told him. "I'm really sorry." Of all the kids at
school, she was the only one who did that. Just looked him
in the eye and said it.

●   ●   ●

The library closed at five. He got a ride home from Naomi's father, Reverend Torvald, who cleared a pile of pamphlets off the backseat to make room for him. Nate had heard that the reverend gave them out door-to-door, telling people how they could keep from going to hell. Nate would never have imagined that Naomi, with all her crazy cartoon drawings and eager, excited bouncing, would have a dried-up old guy like Reverend Torvald—who talked in a monotone and had a "Prayer is the Answer" sticker on his bumper—for a father. The apple could fall far from the tree in some cases, evidently.

Nate told Naomi's dad that it was okay to drop him off at the end of the driveway. "Remember, Nathan," Reverend Torvald said as Nate climbed out, "Jesus loves you."

It was lucky Naomi's father hadn't driven right up to his house. For the second time that week, a police car was parked out front.

Ten

THE OFFICER SITTING IN THE KITCHEN HAD SET UP A portable typewriter on the table. The box of chocolates Nate's grandparents had brought over sat on the lazy Susan—open, with several chocolates missing and pieces of the gold foil Junie liked to use for art projects scattered over the table. Across from the policeman, his mother sat in her apron, her back very straight.

"This is Officer Scruggs, Nathan," she said quietly.

"I'll just change my ribbon here," Officer Scruggs said, stuffing another one of his mother's special chocolates in his mouth. "Maybe your son can go watch TV with that little girl of yours. If he's anything like my boy, all he wants to do is sit around the boob tube, anyway, right?" He made a sound like a laugh.

Nate moved to the refrigerator to get a glass of milk, his daily after-school snack. He reached for the jar of chocolate powder to stir in—imagining, for a second, that he was

brave enough to throw the milk on the police officer and
laugh back. Instead, he walked out of the kitchen, without
comment, in the direction of the TV room. But just because
he'd left didn't mean he couldn't hear. He stood in the hall,
listening.

"Let me get this straight, Mrs. Chance," the policeman
said. "You claim that your husband was depressed about
some kind of crop failure and that it didn't entirely surprise
you that he'd want to take his own life. And how would you
describe your attitude toward your husband in the weeks
and days leading up to the shooting?"

"My attitude?" she said. "I don't know what you mean."

"Would you describe your marriage as happy?"

"Happy? I don't see how that's any of your business,
Officer."

Nate strained to hear. The words "take his own life"
sounded almost like some procedure in a science textbook,
explaining the dissection of a planaria or the insertion of a
pipette in a Bunsen burner. The words didn't match the
meaning.

From where he was leaning against the wall, Nate could
see the photograph of his parents on their wedding day—
his mom in the same dress she still put on for parent-
teacher conferences, his dad in a suit, with the pants too
short and his wrists showing—in front of the old Dodge. His
dad's arm was around his mom, and he was grinning like

the Cubs had just won the World Series. They'd gotten married at the town hall in Roundup and come home right after. Dad was working on Poppa's ranch back then, and chores didn't go away just because someone got married.

"Who needs a honeymoon?" his father had told Nate and Junie one time when she asked where they'd gone after the wedding. "Every day with your mother is a honeymoon."

But then Nate remembered a time, a couple of years back, when his dad had called to him and Junie to come out to the barn. He had a surprise for them, he said. He called it their zipline—a pulley, rigged to the rafters at the highest point in the hayloft. The idea was to climb up on a ladder, grab tight to the handles he'd made, and let yourself sail down the rope, from one end of the barn clear to the other, landing on a big pile of hay.

Even though he was the big brother, Nate was uneasy about trying the zipline. It was Junie who couldn't wait to ride it. "She's pretty little, Dad," Nate had said dubiously. "Are you sure it's okay?"

"She's a trouper," their father replied. "Aren't you, Juniper girl?"

Nate had stood on the straw-covered floor, watching her. She couldn't have been more than four at the time, in her old overalls and her precious pink cowboy boots. "Watch me go, Natie," she called out as she grabbed on to the handles.

Maybe because she weighed so little, she'd taken off so

fast, like some circus performer on *The Ed Sullivan Show*. But her cries were happy ones as she whipped across the barn, high above the cows in their stalls and the cream separator and the buckets.

As she was coming down for a landing, they saw—in the split second before she touched ground—that there was nothing in place to slow her down.

"Junie!" their father yelled, holding his arms out to break her landing, but it was too late. She slammed into the side of the barn wall, hard, and dropped to the ground like a bird hitting a window.

For a moment she just lay there, no sound coming out of her. When she finally cried, they ran to her. "I'm sorry, Junebug," Nate's dad kept saying. Over and over, "I'm sorry."

He carried her into the house, her head cradled in his arms and her cowboy boots dangling. By then she wasn't wailing so much as whimpering. "It's okay, Daddy," she said. "It wasn't your fault."

When their mother saw Junie—blood on her overalls, blood in her hair—she shrieked. First she was all over Junie, of course. But once it was clear that she was okay—her arm probably broken, but otherwise okay—their mom had turned her fury on their dad.

"You're a fool, Carl," she screamed. "I told you not to build that crazy thing. You and your big ideas."

"I'm sorry," Dad said quietly. "I made a mistake."

"I'm tired of your mistakes," she said. "I'm tired of your big ideas and how the rest of us keep paying for them."

Seeing them that way, Junie had lifted her head up from the couch. "Don't fight," she said. "It wasn't Daddy's fault. I just forgot to slow down."

"Look at her, Carl," their mother said, and Nate could hear a change in her voice, a tone he wasn't accustomed to. "You've got your four-year-old daughter making excuses for you."

Their father had closed his eyes.

"Times like this," she said, her voice ice, "I actually think I hate you." She had slapped his face then, though as soon as she did, she burst into tears.

Nate's father put his arms around her.

After, they'd taken Junie to the hospital to set the bone. The whole way into town, nobody spoke, except for one time, when Junie whispered, "It's okay, Daddy. I love you no matter what."

In the hallway Nate drew in his breath quietly to keep from being heard.

"I understand from my talks with your farmhand that you and your husband fought a good deal, Mrs. Chance," the police officer said. "I understand that on some occasions you actually slapped him." From the sound of Officer Scruggs's voice, Nate figured he had another chocolate in his mouth.

No answer.

"And what were you doing the morning of the shooting, Mrs. Chance?"

"Washing the breakfast dishes. Putting fresh sheets on the beds. Working on a new piano piece for the spring recital."

"And would there be any witnesses to attest to that?"

"I was alone all morning. The only people who are around during the day are Carl and Rufus, and they were off working."

"And what about your husband's gun? You didn't notice it was missing from the rack?"

"No."

From the couch in the TV room, Junie was calling out her answers along with the players on *The Match Game*. Nate could hear the sound of Rufus's truck outside, pulling in the driveway for the evening milking. He heard the hum of the refrigerator and the voice of a game-show contestant, talking about what she was planning to do with her prize money. Inside Nate's head there was a ringing sound. He felt the sting of tears.

"Let's just say that if it was me that got taken away, dripping blood," the police officer said, "I'd like to think my wife would show a little concern."

"There's lots of different ways a person can grieve," Nate's mother said quietly. "You don't know anything about what I might be feeling."

Nate stood very still, barely breathing. His cheek was damp, but wiping it would have required him to raise his hand, and he couldn't move.

"When a person shoots himself," the policeman said, "we've got ourselves a gun. You'd think that wherever it was he got shot, that's where his rifle would be lying. Now, I've had my men combing the fields, and it's no place to be found. That's mighty strange."

"What are you saying?" His mother's voice was a whisper.

"I'll be honest with you, Mrs. Chance. Nobody's ruling out the possibility that the one who shot your husband might have been you."

Nate imagined what he'd like to do: tear into the kitchen, punch the guy in his ugly mouth—which would probably be stuffed with chocolates. Pick up his typewriter and throw it through the window.

Only he was fourteen years old. He couldn't make anything happen. All the power in the world seemed to belong to other people: the ones who took his dad away in the first place, the ones who knew where his dad was but wouldn't tell him, the parents—like Larry's mom and dad—who told their children not to talk to him anymore, and now this guy, who was acting like his mother was up on the witness stand.

He could hear the policeman's chair scraping across the linoleum, his mother clearing away his coffee cup. It sounded like Officer Scruggs was finally leaving. His voice, so hard and accusing a moment earlier, returned to its bland, friendly tone.

"I hope you understand, ma'am. It's nothing personal. When allegations have been made, it's my responsibility as an officer of the law to investigate every possibility."

"If you really want to know what happened that day," his mom said, "why don't you ask my husband?"

"Your husband isn't exactly making sense at the moment."

"And just because he can't tell you different, you assume I fired the rifle myself?"

"I'm not saying yes, and I'm not saying no. But if you're asking, are you a suspect for attempted murder, the answer would have to be yes, ma'am, you are."

As soon as the policeman had shut the door, Nate came into the kitchen and sat down across from his mother. Her head lay flat on her arm against the table, and her red hair hid her face.

"Mom." The kitchen had grown dark, and she hadn't gotten up to turn on the lights. Nate could smell something burning on the stove and went to turn off the heat.

"Please, can we talk about Dad?" he asked, sitting down again.

She lifted her head as if it were being pulled by a thread that could barely hold it up and too much sudden motion might make the whole thing snap. She looked in her cup, then out the window, then back in her cup.

"Your father shot himself in the head," she said at last, her words a whisper. "And now, in case that's not enough, the police are saying it might have been me who did it."

"Then we have to go see him. Is he in the hospital?"

"Yes."

"We have to go talk to him."

"He's not in his right mind, Nate. I saw him on that first day, and I don't plan on going back. I can't bear it."

Nate drew in his breath. "Maybe he needs to see us."

"He's in no state for visiting," she told him.

"I'd talk to him," Nate said. "He'd listen to me. Once I talk to him, he'll explain things to the police."

"I don't want to discuss this, Nathan. It's just not the time for going to the hospital."

"When will it be?"

"I don't know."

"It's not fair," he said. His voice was rising. "You think this is just your problem, but it's not. Maybe you don't feel like seeing Dad, but Junie and I do. Don't we count?"

"You don't understand," his mother said. "Your father doesn't have anything for you now. Not for you or your sister or me or anyone."

"It's not about getting anything from him," Nate told her. "Maybe Junie and I just want to help him."

"I wish he'd shown half the compassion for the two of you that you have for him," she said, and there was a bitter sound to her voice that he hated.

"One thing's for sure," Nate told her. "I'm glad I'm not like you. You don't even care what happens to him."

"Don't tell me what I care about."

"Well, not Dad, that's for sure. The policeman was right about that part."

His mother closed her eyes. Very slowly, she shook her head, the way a person might who was seeing something terrible on the news—the scene of an earthquake or some village in Africa where people were starving—but couldn't do anything about it.

"I miss your dad too," she said softly.

"So let's go be with him."

"Right now the most important thing I can do is make sure you and your sister are taken care of," she told him, and her voice was suddenly different. "That's something your father didn't seem to think about much. To me, what he did was not just an act of violence against himself. It was an act of violence against all of us."

Nate got up from the table. "Dad loves us."

"Your dad shot himself in the head, Nate," she said, looking him in the eye finally. "He abandoned us. That's the most selfish thing a parent can do."

"I don't care," he told her, his voice rising again. "I

just want to go see him. I want to know he's okay."

"Well, the truth is, he's not okay. He's lying in a hospital bed with bandages on his head, talking like a crazy person. He can't even manage to shoot himself without messing it up."

"Maybe you can just forget about him, but Junie and I can't."

Nate ran upstairs to his room. Even with the door closed, he could hear his mother downstairs, crying. Lying on his bed, he did the same.

Nate couldn't be sure, but he thought the ambulance that took his father away had the name of a hospital in Leopold on it. So he found the number for that hospital in the phone book in his parents' bedroom and waited till his mother was outside in the barn before making the call.

"Carl Chance," he said. "I'm looking for Carl Chance. I think he might be a patient there."

"Nobody here by that name," the voice said.

He tried the hospital in Beulah next, and then Billings, but nothing. "Maybe he's been released and gone home," one voice told him.

"He isn't home," Nate said.

"I'm sorry," said the voice. "Good luck finding him."

Across the hall the bath was running—Mom getting Junie ready for bed, Junie asking for a story, Mom saying, wearily, "Not tonight, honey. I've got a headache."

"I know what," Junie said. "This time I'll tuck you in for a change." Then came Junie softly humming. She would be stroking her mother's hair, the way she liked to. "Pretty mommy," she said. "Pretty, pretty mommy."

"I'm so sorry, Junie," their mother murmured.

When Nate could tell Junie was in bed—Herman's Hermits playing, as usual—he stepped into her room. He lay down on top of her rodeo bedspread for a long time, stretched out next to his little sister, listening to her breathing become steadier as she finally drifted into sleep.

Eleven

"I GAVE OUT EVERY SINGLE ONE OF MY INVITATIONS,"
Junie told Nate on their way downstairs the next morning.
Their mother was at the stove making pancakes with
bananas, Nate's favorite. She was still in her bathrobe.
Seeing that, anyone who knew her would understand she
wasn't her normal self. One thing they could always count
on was her being dressed and pretty, her pearl necklace on
and her hair curled, by the time they came downstairs a
little before seven.

"Are you sick, Mom?" Junie asked. "Because if you are,
you better get well by my party."

"I'm fine, honey," she said, placing a stack of pancakes
on Junie's plate. "And anyway, your party's practically a
month away. We've got loads of time to prepare."

"I didn't leave a single person out. Even Lynnette."
Lynnette Overbeck was the girl with cerebral palsy who
came to their school, even though she couldn't really do the

work. She was several years older than Junie—tall as Nate, practically. She chewed the collar of her dress so much, there was always a big wet circle around her neck, and sometimes she didn't remember to go to the bathroom. But Junie was always nice to her.

"I bet the kids were excited, huh?" said their mother. Nate studied her with a hard, cold eye, like how he'd look at someone he'd just met. He could see her trying hard to act normal.

"Uh-huh," said Junie. "I told them what I want for my present. Model horses for my collection or a miniature stable or sparkly jewelry or a Barbie convertible."

"That's good, honey."

All of a sudden, every single thing his mother was doing got on Nate's nerves, like how she kept stacking pancakes on his plate, even though he still had plenty.

"I told them we were making a really special cake," Junie said. "But I didn't give away the surprise of it being in the shape of a circus tent. I don't want anyone to find out till they get here."

"Listen, J," Nate said, putting his fork down. "I've been meaning to talk to you about this party of yours. It could turn out that not so many people show up."

"What are you talking about, silly? I invited my whole class. And a bunch of others besides."

"It's just that sometimes people can act weird. Some

people might have dumb ideas about our family and tell their kids they can't come to your party or something."

His mother looked up from the stove. "What are you talking about, Nate?"

"I'm talking about what's really going on. Unlike every single other person in this family."

"Nathan." She reached for his arm, but he pushed her away.

"You know what?" he said. "You just plain don't care about Dad. I don't even know what to believe happened anymore."

She raised her hand, like she was going to slap him, but she did something else. She slapped her self instead, hard enough to leave a mark on her own cheek.

"Look who's crazy now," he yelled over the sound of her weeping. The fact that she was crying only made him madder. He was dimly aware of his sister, wrapping herself around their mother's waist.

There was a tall stack of pancakes on his plate, with syrup dripping down the sides. He lifted the plate off the table and held it up. Then he dumped the whole thing on the floor and ran out of the house.

"Natie," his sister called after him. "Natie, come back."

"My word, Nathan," Aunt Sal said when he stepped into her kitchen, breathing hard. "What are you doing here on a school day?" She was taking bread out of the oven. "Look at you. Not even a coat on. You'll catch your death."

"I need to talk to you," he said. "I need to talk about Dad."

She set down the loaf, put a towel over it, and pulled out a chair. She poured a glass of milk and set it on the table in front of him. "I know," she said. "Your mom just called."

At the word "mom," Nate began to cry. He cried and cried, unable to stop. He cried so hard, he could barely breathe, so hard that the tears made his eyes sting and everything around him was a blur, like being in a car in a thunderstorm with the windshield wipers broken. It was a long time before he could speak, but Aunt Sal just sat there, with her arms around him, waiting.

"I hate her," he wept. "I hate how she acts like nothing even happened. I hate how she doesn't even care."

"Your mom cares plenty," his aunt said at last. "She just doesn't know what to do. Your dad's very sick. Yesterday he was transferred to the psychiatric hospital in Warm Springs."

"I don't care if he's sick," Nate said. "I need to see him."

"I wish you could understand that your mom is doing the best she can," Aunt Sal said. "It was bad enough, her seeing him. She doesn't want you to get upset."

"Not seeing him is what upsets me," Nate told her. "Don't you get it?"

She fingered the tablecloth. "Then there's your grandfather to consider," she said. "You have to understand, he's one of those people who don't have a lot of tolerance for human weakness. Poppa and Grandma lived through the Great Depression, and as far as they're concerned, anyone with a roof over his head and a little food in his belly has nothing to complain about. Your grandpa used just about every penny of his life savings to buy that piece of land for your mom and dad and this other section here for your uncle Harold and me. In his eyes we should all be happy, and anyone who's not is just not trying hard enough. Right now it's looking like your mom may lose the farm, and your grandpa's doing everything he can to keep that from happening. He has no use for your father."

Nate thought about his father working long days, into darkness even, herding their cows back from the grazing land, the blisters on his hands from weeks of baling hay. "It's not Dad's fault, he just had bad luck."

Aunt Sal got up from the table. She took out a long bread knife and cut two slices from the fresh loaf. She spread butter over them. One piece for him, one for her. "Technically, I'm not supposed to cut into this till it's completely cool, but I'm making an exception," she said. "On account of you're my favorite nephew."

They ate their bread in silence, but it was a comfortable kind of silence.

"It's no fair being a kid," Nate told her. "Everything important that happens is some grown-up's decision."

"I'd take you to Warm Springs myself to see him if I could, but your grandpa would never forgive me."

"Dad needs us." He didn't add the other part: He needed his dad too.

"Try to be patient, Nate. Just give your mom a little time. We'll work things out, I promise."

It was close to noon by the time Nate left Aunt Sal and Uncle Harold's house. There wasn't much point in going to school, even if he could have gotten there, and he wasn't in the mood to see his mother yet. He stood on the edge of their land and looked out over the flat expanse of snow. More had fallen since the shooting, which had made the search for the gun difficult. Still, he paced the land like a soldier, on the unlikely chance his boot might hit the butt of the rifle or his eye catch sight of the nose sticking up through a snowdrift. He searched that way all afternoon, till the sun hung low on the horizon, when he realized the gun could be lying right on top of a snowbank and still he wouldn't see it. Then he headed slowly home.

Often, coming toward the house at this hour, he'd hear the sound of his mother playing the piano, but today there was nothing. Inside, she sat at the kitchen table with the check register and a cup of coffee.

When she saw Nate in the doorway, she got up. "I'm sorry, honey," she said, and opened her arms like she was going to put them around him.

He couldn't meet her embrace.

"Nate," she began. But whatever she was going to say, she didn't say it. He didn't answer. He simply walked past her and upstairs to his room, then closed the door behind him.

Twelve

NATE TOLD HIMSELF HE WASN'T GOING TO CARE ABOUT the science fair. Just blow it off, get a passing grade. Only he couldn't help caring. Sitting in English class while the teacher droned on about the *Odyssey*, he drew sketches of the cloud chamber and made a list of all the materials he'd need to build it. Even though Naomi was officially his partner, he still liked to think of the project as his alone.

Most of the items—sheets of glass, glue, rubber stripping, blotting paper, flat black spray paint, a flashlight, masking tape, tongs—were things he could find in the implement shed or scrounge around for on his own. But there were a couple of things—dry ice and ethyl alcohol—that he needed to order from a scientific supply house. There was an address for one printed in the back of his magazine.

He also had to locate something that would serve as the radioactive source inside the chamber, for their control test.

A glow-in-the-dark watch face—a radium dial from back in the olden days—seemed like the answer. There was his dad's, of course, but Nate assumed he was wearing it the day they took him away.

At breakfast Mom spooned out the oatmeal. Once again she was in her bathrobe. Neither of them had said anything more since he'd come home yesterday, but now he had to talk to her. It was one of the humiliating things he hated about being a kid: You couldn't even be mad at your parents all that long, because you always needed their help with something—a ride or a signature on a permission slip or, like he did now, money.

"The science fair is coming up at school. I need some money. It's for the cloud chamber I'm building. I need to send away for some stuff."

"Oh, Nathan," his mom said. "I wish I could help, but money's so tight at the moment. Can't you choose a project where you use the things we've got on hand?"

"It's a really special project. I'll pay you back."

She sighed. "I don't know what we're going to do. That loan your dad took out is way past due, and I can't pay it."

"If only I could ride Bucky," said Junie. "I could get a paper route and deliver the newspaper on horseback. We could even do an act and enter the rodeo and win a prize."

"That pony is good for nothing," their mother said wearily.

"I'm training him," Junie said. "You wait and see. I'm getting him calmed down to where I can ride him. He just needs to get used to life around here a little more. It was just so hard where he was living before."

"Before he got to Easy Street," Mom said with a sad little laugh.

"Bucky loves our family," Junie told her. "He's going to be like a regular, normal pony before you know it. All he needs is a little more love."

"I don't want to disappoint you, Junie, but it doesn't usually work that way with an animal that's experienced a lot of abuse."

"Anyway," said Junie, "I don't even care if I can ride him. I just love him, is all."

"Love's all very well," Mom said, "but it doesn't pay the bills." She picked up the laundry basket and headed out to the line to bring in the clothes, leaving Nate's question about money for supplies unanswered. It was just one more thing he'd have to figure out on his own.

In science, Nate let Naomi be the one to give Mrs. Unger the rundown on their cloud chamber. As she talked, he could see Pauline Calhoun and her friend Jennifer imitating the excited little gestures Naomi made and how she twisted her hair. Pauline jingled her bracelet and flashed Larry a look. He grinned.

After Naomi was finished, Mrs. Unger told the class they could spend the period working on their projects. Nate watched Larry and Travis lean toward each other at their side-by-side desks, laughing and talking. Already, in the space of a few days, it looked like Travis had totally taken over the role of Larry's best friend.

Naomi pulled up her chair next to Nate's and started looking for a pencil. She dumped the contents of one of her book bags on his desk: a dried-up Magic Marker, a hairbrush, a sock, a headband, a half-eaten candy bar. A leather notebook with a rubber band around it fell out, and a piece of paper with what looked to be a poem scribbled down. "It's a song by Bob Dylan I heard on the radio," she explained. "'Mr. Tambourine Man.' Some people might think it doesn't make any sense, but to me, it's the most perfect song I ever heard."

This is hopeless, Nate thought. He had to deal with a science partner who carried around gunk-encrusted M&M's and some weird song that made no sense. How was a person like that ever going to focus on mitering corners or tracking alpha rays?

"So," she said, "I was thinking we should read up a little on the history of scientific attitudes toward the stars over the centuries. Just for a little historical perspective, you know?"

"Whatever," he said.

A few minutes before the bell Mrs. Unger asked if any-one cared to share with the class how their work was going. Loretta Foster raised her hand. "I've been studying the rela-tionship between the sense of smell and the taste buds," she said. "Last night I had my dad hold his nose while he chewed on a piece of potato and a piece of apple, and he couldn't tell the difference."

"Sounds interesting, Loretta," Mrs. Unger said.

"Maybe all you proved is that your dad's crazy," said Eddie.

"My dad is a really smart person," said Loretta, who was an unusually humorless person. "I'll have you know he was named Salesman of the Year at Robinson Chevy Oldsmobile two years in a row."

A few seats over, Kirk leaned across the aisle. "Yeah, well, a person can crack up anytime," he whispered. "You never know when Loretta's dad might be paying a visit to you-know-who over at the loony bin."

"Boys," Mrs. Unger said, "I don't want to have to sepa-rate your desks, but if the chatter continues, I'll have no choice."

A number of kids—the ones who'd heard what Kirk had said—looked at Nate for a reaction. So did Mrs. Unger. Luckily, the bell rang then. People gathered up their back-packs and got to their feet. Just outside the door, Naomi caught up with him.

"Know what I do when someone acts like that to me?" she said. "I draw a really funny picture of them with all their worst features exaggerated. I just ask myself, would I want to be friends with someone as mean as that?"

The truth was, Nate would.

"Never mind," she told him. "I'm your friend."

It was hard to say if that was good news or not.

The next week Nate and Naomi were sitting in the cafeteria, having lunch again. Nate was coming to accept the fact that if he wanted company at lunch, Naomi was it.

"Where should we work today?" she asked, unwrapping her awful-looking egg salad sandwich.

By now they'd established a sort of routine. If they were working on the written report portion of their project, they'd meet at the library after school, and later Nate would catch a ride home with Jed Landry. Jed had a job at the diner that got out just when the library closed, and unlike most people, he didn't seem to treat Nate like he had some kind of contagious disease.

Now that they were gearing up for the actual construction of the cloud chamber, though, Naomi would come over to Nate's house. He'd cleared the worktable in the implement shed for the two of them. He didn't mind Naomi seeing his messed-up family, probably because he knew that she had her own embarrassing family stuff to deal with.

She'd told Nate that one time, when she'd gotten home late, her father had taken his strap to her.

"It's not that big a deal," she'd said. "He does it a lot."

"Even when my dad's been in really bad shape, he never hit one of us," Nate told her. "And my mom, no way." He didn't tell her about the time he'd seen her slap his dad.

"My dad believes that if you spare the rod, you spoil the child," Naomi said. "But one thing's for sure. If I have kids someday, I'm never going to hit them."

He and Naomi had figured the materials they needed to buy for the cloud chamber would add up to twenty-four dollars, not counting the postage fee. He had thirteen silver dollars saved up from what Poppa gave him every birthday. Naomi said she could make up the difference with babysitting money.

It was funny how this worked. Four times now, Nate had shoplifted baseball cards at the five-and-ten, but when it came to getting the money for their project materials, it seemed like he had to do it fair and square. After school that day he and Naomi pooled their money and walked over to the bank. They bought a money order and mailed it off to the scientific supply house in Chicago, along with the order for dry ice and the rest of the items they had to purchase.

"While we're waiting for our materials to come," Naomi said, "we can build the box."

At first it had bothered Nate, the way she seemed to view herself as a totally equal partner in the project, instead of what he'd pictured her as—more of a lab assistant. But now he thought that was a nice thing about her, actually. She wasn't one of those girls who stood around giggling and waiting for the boy to do everything.

The two of them were in the implement shed, where the pieces for the cloud chamber were spread out. Watching Naomi laboring at his dad's old workbench, Nate thought about times he and his father had built things here: their ship in a bottle, their ant farm, the walkie-talkies they'd rigged up that actually allowed a person in the barn to talk to someone in the house.

Naomi was bent over the diagram in the magazine and another one they'd found in a book from the library. "This business about putting in a depressurizing gauge has me confused," she said. "They say here you need it, but in the other version you don't."

When he'd first read about the pressure gauge and saw how complicated it was, Nate thought they should just leave that part out. After all, it didn't matter if they did a great job. But now, hearing her question, he said the first thing that came into his head.

"If my dad was here, he'd know how to rig it up."

"So what's going on?" Naomi asked him. "Where is your dad, anyway?"

There it was all of a sudden—the simplest question, and it had taken so long for anyone to ask it. Nate felt a rush of appreciation. Why was it so hard for people to say what they were really thinking?

"He's at a mental hospital in Warm Springs," Nate told her. "But my mom won't let us visit. She thinks it would upset us or something."

"Grown-ups have some strange ideas about what's best for kids, don't they? Like we can't figure out what's going on, just because we're young."

"It's funny how they're so anxious to protect us all of a sudden," Nate said. "Back before it happened, my dad was doing a lot of crazy stuff, and nobody seemed to care if we saw it."

"I know what you mean," she said. "My mother's always so concerned I might read one little word in a book she doesn't approve of, like a character saying a swear or some-thing. But does she mind if my dad hits me so hard it leaves a mark?"

They didn't say anything for a while then. He held up a sheet of glass that was meant to form the base for the cloud chamber. She uncapped the glue.

"So what are you going to do about your dad?" Naomi asked him. "You can't just wait around forever. If it was me, I'd want to see him right now."

Thirteen

NATE FIGURED IT WAS ABOUT THREE HUNDRED MILES from Lonetree to Warm Springs. He could hitchhike, except everyone in town knew him, and he doubted they'd pick him up. Even if they did, the first thing they'd ask would be: *Does your mom know about this?*

There was a bus—he'd checked—but the same thing could happen. Someone would see him and ask what he was doing, traveling so far on his own. It was one of the problems about living in a small town.

Every Saturday the spur line of the railroad came through Lonetree to haul away the feed in the grain elevators. The thought came to Nate that he could hop a freight, like hoboes used to do. It was nothing he'd ever tried, though he and Larry used to lay pennies on the tracks for the train to flatten or lie alongside the tracks, imagining that they'd jump on board when it came by.

Friday night Nate packed his provisions—a turkey

sandwich wrapped up in a bandana, a bottle of soda, and his one remaining silver dollar that he'd kept for emergencies. The depot where the spur line stopped lay about a mile and a half from their land. It came in the mornings, but he hadn't ever paid that close attention to when exactly. Never mind—he'd get there early enough that he'd be ready.

The day was surprisingly warm for March. He didn't need his heavy jacket—just a sweatshirt. He stuck his paper with the first hundred and fifty digits of pi in his pocket, along with a joke book Junie had given him for his last birthday, to keep himself occupied on the trip.

Stepping out the back door in the predawn light, he could feel his heart beating hard. He thought about all the mornings he and his dad had risen early like this to head out on one of their adventures. This was the first time it was just Nate on his own.

The night before, Nate had told his mom he was going out early to help Larry with his paper route. If she'd been paying more attention, she would have noticed that Larry never called him anymore. But she just nodded and said fine. She almost looked relieved that she wouldn't have to deal with him at breakfast.

He hadn't expected to bump into Rufus, who pulled up in his old Chevy just as Nate was heading down the road. Even before the shooting, Nate had never liked Rufus.

"Up pretty early," Rufus said, leaning out the window of the cab.

"I'm going to see someone."

"Walking, huh? Too bad that bike of yours ain't roadworthy. I was always telling your dad we should just haul that thing over to the dump. You'd think he would've done something about it."

Nate had had the same thought, but hearing Rufus say it made his back stiffen. "My dad and me were going to build a dirt bike together." *Are.* He should have said "are going to."

"Oh. Right." Rufus's lip curled into something that looked, to Nate, like a sneer.

"You know how to build a dirt bike, Rufus?" Nate asked him.

"No."

"Well, my dad does." He turned his back and walked off.

Nate had left himself a good forty-five minutes for the hike, with plenty of margin in case the train loaded up and took off earlier than he thought. On the road he imagined how it would be if his plan actually worked and he managed to hop the freight and ride it clear to Anaconda, then hitchhike to Warm Springs. How he'd locate the hospital and how he'd get in to see his dad. Knowing they had him in a mental ward, he wondered if there'd be guards or locks on the doors. He pictured himself climbing up a fire escape, prying open a window, making off with an orderly suit, and acting like he worked there.

Tromping along the road—past the Landrys' barn, the mailboxes, the old abandoned windmill—Nate tried to prepare himself for the sight of his dad. He'd be wearing some kind of hospital-type outfit, like one of those tunics the patients wore on *Dr. Kildare.* If he was really acting crazy, they might have him in a straitjacket, with arms buckled against his chest, so he couldn't even feed himself. Nate didn't like to think about that possibility, but it was better than getting caught by surprise.

The sun was barely up when he got to the loading depot. He had seen the spur train come and go enough over the years to have a strategy worked out: He'd wait till the men had assembled on the loading dock, then he'd scramble up onto one of the cars on the other side. He knew to be careful about not ending up in a car with a load of grain pouring down on top of him. That had happened to a boy over in Leopold one time. Better to ride between cars.

Sometime around seven thirty, to judge by the light, the train pulled in. A couple of men began loading the grain into one of the boxcars. Based on the size of the load, Nate figured that in another ten or fifteen minutes they'd be done and he could sneak on board through the opening in a panel on the side.

From the embankment where he waited, he heard a voice.

"Fancy meeting you here." The voice came from a spot by the tracks, a little ways up from where Nate had planted himself.

Looking up, he saw a wiry man in very old clothes, sporting the kind of hat sea captains wore in the movies. His beard was mostly white, and in the place where his right arm should have been there was an empty sleeve, pinned to his shirt.

"You got a name?" the man asked.

"Nate."

"I'm Frank. Thought I was going to have this car to myself. Glad for the company." He took out a little packet of tobacco and rolling papers.

Nate watched with interest as Frank rolled a cigarette, one-handed.

Frank explained that he had come in on another train, three days before. He'd heard there might be temporary work at the broom factory over in Leopold, but no such luck. "Some people get the idea that just because I got one arm less than the usual, I might not be able to keep up," he said. "But never mind. I'll find me a job in Idaho. If not, there's always Washington."

"You travel around a lot like this, huh?" Nate asked him.

"Fifty years, more or less. I was probably about your age first time I took off."

Nate studied his face—his skin the color of dry earth after a long stretch of drought. He tried to imagine Frank his own age but couldn't.

"Let me guess," said Frank. "Your old man gave you a hard time about something, and you're so steamed, you're running away from home."

"I'm just making a little trip over to Anaconda. I'm not running away from anyone."

"First time out?" Frank asked him. Nate wasn't sure what he meant. "Riding the rails, I mean."

"My first time."

"Man, I remember mine," Frank told him. "I was fourteen years old. Before the war. I'm talking about the first one. We lived in Milwaukee back then, in a real house. But I was restless, you know. Caught a case of the wandering bug."

"You ever go back?"

A dreamy look came over Frank's face then. "Can't say I ever saw my mother's face again," he said. "I don't carry a lot of regrets in life, but that is one."

"I'm not leaving home permanently or anything," Nate told him, imagining for a moment how it would be if he'd just said good-bye to his mother forever, instead of for a day. "I'm just going to see someone."

The old man looked at him for a long minute. He was probably around the age of Poppa, but Nate couldn't picture his grandfather admitting to a single wrong move in his life. "And what happens after you find this person?" Frank asked him. "What do you do then?"

"He's in a hospital. I have to make sure he's all right."

Frank drew on his cigarette. "That sounds fair enough," he said. "Except for one problem. You ever think what you'll do if this person ain't all right? Think you can just pack up and git back to where you come from then?"

The truth was, Nate hadn't actually thought about that. When he had pictured this trip, the farthest Nate ever got in his imagining was walking in a room someplace and seeing his dad there. Running to put his arms around him. His father bending down to muss up his hair and reaching in his pocket, maybe, for some crinkled-up article he'd cut out of a magazine about Saturn's rings or cosmic dust. He never pictured the other part—what his dad would tell him about the gun, the shooting, why it happened, what was going to happen now. Or how things would go when he had to say good-bye, had to walk out the door again and head back home.

Frank took another drag on his cigarette and studied Nate closely. "This person you're going to see," he said. "I'm guessing this might be someone pretty close. I'm thinking your old man, maybe?"

Nate nodded. No point lying, when it appeared this guy knew everything already.

"And he's in some kind of trouble, right? And you've taken it upon yourself to make things right."

Nate studied the empty sleeve pinned to one side of Frank's shirt and the weathered fingers of his one hand, holding on to the cigarette. "Something like that."

"Don't get me wrong, buddy," Frank told him. "But maybe your plan needs a little more considering before you make this trip. Maybe you've been so dang busy figuring out how to get to your dad, you haven't got your idea straight— what you're going to accomplish once you're there."

A sick, sad feeling came over Nate then. In a quiet voice he said words he had never spoken before: "My father shot himself, but he didn't die. He's in a mental ward."

After that it all spilled out: his grandfather mad because his dad wasn't strong like him; his mother walking around like a zombie all the time; his little sister trying to make everyone happy; Larry saying they couldn't be friends.

"The police think my mom might have done it because they haven't found the gun. I need to ask my dad where he left his rifle, so they'll stop blaming her. I need to help my dad. I need to be able to come home and tell my sister I saw him and he's okay."

Frank drew long and deep on his cigarette. "Sounds like you've taken it upon yourself to fix everything that's broke in your family right now," he said. "That's a big job for a boy to take on. Big job for anyone."

"I don't know what else to do."

"Let's think about your dad a minute," Frank said. "I'm

guessing the guy don't even know hisself where he left the darn rifle. Guy in that kind of shape probably didn't take no particular mind to latitude and longitude at the time. And if they're saying he ain't making sense, it's likely he won't have a whole heck of a lot to offer on that score."

Nate knew this, actually. He'd figured as much himself. But there was the other part: just wanting to let his dad know how much he and Junie missed him, how much they wanted him back.

"Of course you want to see your dad," Frank went on. "The thing is, what does he need right now that you can give him? If it was me, I'd want to know my kids were doing okay. But first that would have to be true."

Up on the tracks it looked like the men loading the grain were finishing up—meaning that he and Frank should be ready to scramble up the embankment and make their way onto the freight car.

"Maybe you have some things to attend to back home before you head off to Anaconda," Frank told Nate. "You may have to find out a few things yourself before you can be much help to anybody else."

"I always had my dad before. For baseball and stuff. Or like now, when I'm building this science project. We would've done that together. I bet if he was around, I'd even win first prize."

"See what I mean?" said Frank. "What good do you

think you'll be to him, if you show up carrying on about how you can't live without him? Sounds to me like you better build your project and win that prize without your old man. Once you've got something worthwhile to tell him—like how you're going to be all right, so he don't have to worry—that's when you get yourself to the hospital. No point showing up empty-handed."

Nate thought about the diagram he'd cut out from the magazine—how complicated it looked. The way the two sides of the cloud chamber had come unglued when he and Naomi had tried to join them to the base, and one of the pieces of glass had broken.

Nate studied the freight car. All week he'd been planning this trip. He'd pictured how he was going to hop on board. How it would be, scrunched up in the corner, feeling the rumbling of the wheels on the track, and the moment when he stepped outside again, in Anaconda.

"'Course, then you've got a guy like me," Frank went on. "I always said I wouldn't go home till I could give my old lady something to be proud of. Fifty years later I ain't never made it back, and it's not likely she'd still be there waiting if I did."

From over on the tracks, they could hear the low sound of the train engine starting up and the shrill wail of the whistle. Frank lifted himself up off the grass and made his way over to the train car. The door was open just enough to slip inside. Nate considered again how it might be to jump on next to the old man and find himself, a few hours later, pulling into the station in Anaconda. He could get to his father by nightfall. He let his brain imagine how it would feel to hear his father's voice, see his face.

"I'm not telling you it ain't a good idea to go see your dad," Frank said over his shoulder as he pulled himself up so that he was standing alongside of the freight car. "I'm only telling you, first things first."

He scrambled on board then, swinging himself up by his one sinewy arm. "Take care of yourself, chum," Frank called, as the train pulled away, leaving Nate standing there alone on the muddy embankment to make his way back home.

Up until now Nate had been feeling almost resentful of the obligation to complete the science fair project. He could lie on the floor of the implement shed while Naomi fiddled with the sides of the box and the miter saw, and if things didn't work out all that great (which they didn't; she was terrible with tools), who cared?

But walking home, it became clear to him: He would build the cloud chamber not for his teacher or for the fair or for a good grade. He'd build it for his father. He and Naomi would make the most amazing science fair project the judges had ever seen.

He imagined the moment, six weeks from now, when the whole junior high school would be assembled in the gymnasium with their projects set out for the judges, and the principal and Mrs. Unger would be up onstage in front of the microphones. He saw his mother standing there—dressed up like she used to be when there was a special event at school—and his little sister beaming. She'd be so excited, he'd need to remind her to stand still. Naomi would be wearing one of her rumpled dresses, but never mind.

And the winner is . . . , he could hear Mrs. Unger saying. Then his name and Naomi's would come over the loud-speaker.

Up on the stage his teacher would hand them the trophy—the biggest he'd ever seen, not that this would stop him from lifting it high over his head. As he did, he'd see Larry, nodding and clapping, like he was sorry for how he'd acted, and the face of Pauline Calhoun twisted like an evil witch, gnashing her teeth before stomping out of the gymnasium. He'd watch his mother's face burst into a smile again. His little sister would scream like girls did when the Beatles were on *Ed Sullivan.* The whole crowd would be cheering—cheering and smiling. *We were wrong about you, Nate,* the principal would say as he shook his hand. *We owe you and your whole family an apology.*

Then all of them—he and his sister and their mom—would get in the car and sweep off to Warm Springs, and when they got there, his dad would be waiting for them, and they would all be together again.

Maybe not that part. Nate knew, of course, that wasn't very likely. But he would make the trip anyway—he and Junie. And he would tell his dad about the cloud chamber and show him the trophy.

I'm so proud of you, son, his dad would say. And a look would come over his father's face that Nate hadn't seen in a long time. Happiness.

Fourteen

SPRING WAS STARTING TO COME TO LONETREE. Baseball tryouts—always the best thing about this time of year—would happen soon. With the snow beginning to melt, planting season was upon them, but nobody in Nate's family was saying anything about that. All his mother and his grandfather did lately was go over the books of the farm, the mounting pile of unpaid bills, Sam Carter's overdue loan note shoved to the bottom. With no customers left to buy their cream, milk soured in the buckets. The wind whipped the loose shutters on the house that no one had gotten around to repairing. It had been weeks since he'd heard his mom play the piano.

"Maybe we can find someone to lease our land till I get on my feet, Dad, and I'd take a percentage of the yield for the three of us to live on," he'd overheard his mother say one night recently. Poppa and Grandma and Aunt Sal and

Uncle Harold had stopped by for dinner, and everyone supposed he was safely upstairs, working on his homework.

"You know that would never pay the bills, Helen," Poppa told her. "Small farm like this, Carl had a hard enough time getting the place to support one family, never mind two."

"I could get a job in town," she said. "Clerk over at Morton's, maybe. Or wait on tables at the steak house."

"You don't think people talk enough as it is?" Nate's grandmother said to her.

"At least I wouldn't have to sit around at home waiting for another policeman to knock at the door."

"If we could only find Carl's rifle," Aunt Sal said.

It was out there somewhere. Instead of getting ready for baseball tryouts when the bus let him off after school, Nate would choose a section of field and pace its length, hoping to catch sight of it. But for all his searching—the hours he spent walking their land, eyes to the ground—it seemed as if the earth had simply opened up and swallowed the thing.

The rest of the time, he and Naomi worked on their science fair project. Ideas for how to make it better came to him at odd times throughout the day and even in the night. Shortly after his talk with Frank, Nate had revised his thought about not needing a depressurizing gauge for the cloud chamber. Since then they'd been struggling to make theirs work, without compromising the seal on the chamber itself. He'd called Naomi up one night at nine thirty—late enough to wake her dad—to tell her a new idea.

"I've been worried the flashlight beam just won't be strong enough to make the tracks of the alpha and beta rays show up," he said. "But I figured out what our light source can be. My uncle's slide projector." He said it like some old-time prospector who'd just found gold in his pan.

"What's got into you, anyway?" Naomi asked him the next day. They were sitting in the cafeteria together, and he was talking about how it would be, once they had the dry ice and they could run their actual test.

"I just decided we're going to have the best science fair project ever, that's all," he told her.

Even though the science fair was still more than a month away, every day that they had to refine their cloud chamber suddenly seemed precious.

Naomi was in charge of the written report and the drawings for their poster. Both of them worked on the actual construction of the cloud chamber, but Naomi understood that was more Nate's department. He wanted the box to be perfect before they did their dry run. At the moment they had glue drying on the rubber seals, and nothing much could be done until it set. And the dry ice had to come from Chicago—something that needed to happen as close to the date of the science fair as possible.

"This is going to be so cool," Naomi told Nate as they

sat together on the bus heading home after school. In the seat behind her, Junie was braiding Naomi's hair and putting plastic barrettes in it. Another girl—someone like Pauline Calhoun—would never have let Junie do something that made her look funny, but Naomi didn't mind. "Be my guest," she'd said the first time Junie asked if she could try out a new hairdo on Naomi. "Anything would be an improvement."

"I guess you don't need me to come over for anything today," Naomi said. She was showing Nate a bunch of cartoons she'd drawn of their teachers, which looked almost as good as what the artists in *Mad* magazine did.

"You could come over anyway, if you feel like it," he told her. "Just to hang around. It's not like I've got anything so pressing on my schedule."

The last few weeks they had been selling off cows, and he missed the old familiar rounds of milking and cleaning out the stalls in the barn. With less livestock to tend, and even less money, his mom had let Rufus go, though he still came by now and then to lend a hand, in exchange for an old engine they'd had out in the shed that Nate's mom gave him.

"Nothing on my social calendar either," Naomi said. "Pauline's having a bunch of girls over to her house tonight to try on makeup and sleep over, but big surprise, I'm not included."

•　　•　　•

"Hey, I have the new Beatles album," Nate told Naomi as they climbed off the bus together. "We could go up to my room and listen to it." His aunt Sal had bought it for him in Billings last week—*Revolver.* The record jacket had the most fascinating picture—a line drawing of the four of them, with all kinds of characters and images hidden in their hair and twisting around the sides of the picture. Nate had spent hours studying the drawing while he lay on his bed listening to the lyrics of the songs. Naomi had shown him her own version of the *Revolver* cover, only instead of the Beatles, it featured members of the eighth grade at Lonetree Junior High.

Poppa said it was a waste of time, listening to a bunch of mop-tops who had nothing better to do than sing about love. But when Nate's mom had heard the album, she'd stood at the top of the stairs listening for a long time. Junie liked "Good Day Sunshine" and "Yellow Submarine." "Eleanor Rigby" made Nate think of his father—the part about all the lonely people.

"So which one is your favorite?" he asked Naomi as she sat studying the record jacket. "Mine's George."

"John, definitely," Naomi said. Nearly all the girls at school were crazy about Paul, especially after his song "Michelle" came out. "I figure John's the most intelligent. And he has this slightly twisted way of looking at things."

"My little sister likes Ringo because he seems so

cheerful," he told her. "She just likes people to be happy all the time."

"That's not really possible, is it?" Naomi told him. "I mean, you'd have to be an idiot."

They sat on the floor in his room, listening to the record all the way through. Sometime in the middle of "Here, There, and Everywhere," Naomi spoke.

"I just want to make one thing clear," she said. "We're not boyfriend-girlfriend material. I don't want to embarrass you, but it seemed like we should get that out on the table."

He studied her face—her large, intense eyes under the thatch of thick bangs, her mouth that seemed big for her face and never stayed still. Her tights had a run, and as usual, her dress was rumpled. He remembered when he used to think she was weird-looking, but the way she appeared to him now was nice, actually. Like someone who wouldn't mind sitting in the barn with the cows.

"I wasn't really in the mood for that type of deal either," he said to her. "I've got enough going on."

"But friends is good," she said. "When you're boyfriend and girlfriend, there's sure to come a time when you break up, and then you've got a mess on your hands. Where friends don't have to end."

He thought of Larry and of the secret pledge they'd made when they were little: *Friends forever.* But mostly, she was right. Friendship might not be foolproof, but it was safer than romance.

"So we've got that straightened out," she said. "That's a relief."

At five o'clock Mrs. Torvald's car pulled up. Hearing her mother pulling down the drive, Naomi jumped up quickly and grabbed her book bags. Nate walked her out to the yard.

"You young scientists find a cure for cancer yet?" Mrs. Torvald asked. She had a way of talking to the two of them like they were six years old. Unlike Naomi's father, who seemed scary to Nate, Naomi's mother seemed gentle enough, but she was also one of those women who acted like her husband was the boss, like she would never understand anything other than cooking and doing laundry. She had never seemed to grasp what their project was about or shown any sign of caring that she didn't.

"One of these days," Nate told Mrs. Torvald as Naomi climbed into the car. In addition to her two home-sewn book bags, Naomi had a stack of loose papers spilling from her arms. She got into the backseat, where there was more room.

Nate stood there in the driveway for a minute. As the car pulled away Naomi turned around to give him a goofy look out the back window. She was crossing her eyes and making circles in the air, the sign for crazy, in the direction of her mom. She pulled out a hank of hair as if an electrical current had run through her and made it stand on end.

He turned and walked back to the house while she could still see him, stiff legged, with his arms out front, like he was Frankenstein. Only, unlike Frankenstein, he was smiling.

Fifteen

OFFICER SCRUGGS WAS BACK. HE SHOWED UP AT THE door as Nate was heading in from the implement shed.

"How's it going, son?" he said. The two of them stepped into the kitchen together.

What was a person supposed to say to that? My dad's in a mental hospital, our farm is going bankrupt, and my mom's under suspicion—by you—for shooting my dad. Otherwise, things are great?

Nate's mother must have known Officer Scruggs was coming, because she'd changed out of her bathrobe. As she poured him a cup of coffee her hand shook—a regular problem these days. She didn't fix herself a cup, just took her seat at the table across from the policeman with a look of weary resignation.

"Go tend to your chores, Nate," she told him. "I need to speak privately with Officer Scruggs." He left the room. But only for his usual spot in the back hall, where he could listen.

"You may not have heard, Mrs. Chance," the policeman began, "but one of our detectives paid another visit to your husband. We'd learned from the doctor up there that in spite of his injuries, he was speaking more lucidly. Our man thought he might get some long-overdue answers concerning the shooting and the whereabouts of the gun."

"So he told you he did it?" Nate's mom said. "He told you, right?"

"He can speak just fine, I'm happy to say," the officer said. "But he says he has no memory of that day. No memory of what happened. Anytime we try to ask him more, it's like a curtain goes down, and he's done talking."

"My husband is a troubled man," she said. "I told you that already."

"He's a man that got shot," Officer Scruggs said. "We just need to find out who did it."

In the hallway Nate leaned against the wall. The good news was, his father could speak. That stuff the women had said at the five-and-ten that day, about him being a vegetable, wasn't true. But evidently, the police were still ready to believe that Nate's mom might have shot his dad.

"So I need to ask you again, Mrs. Chance," the officer said, his spoon clinking against the china cup, "where exactly were you on the morning of the day of the shooting?"

"I've told you this already," she sighed. "I was doing the

same thing I always do, mornings. Making breakfast for my family. Cleaning up. Getting my sheet music organized for a piano lesson."

"And remind me: Where exactly was your husband at this point?"

"My husband didn't usually eat breakfast with the rest of us. Carl was always more of a loner. He'd get up early, read the paper, and head out to the barn or go putter on something in the implement shed. Sometimes I think he just drove around in that truck of his. A lot of the time I never actually knew what he was up to."

"You yourself remained in the house?" Officer Scruggs asked.

"Yes." Exasperation in her voice.

"And would there be witnesses to corroborate that?"

"Only my children."

Nate remembered the day, of course. He'd been back over it a thousand times, trying to imagine how he might have made things turn out different, how he could have kept his dad from doing what he did.

Rufus had been off on a feed run that morning, so Nate and his dad had gotten up before his mother and sister to do the milking. They seldom talked much anymore, but Nate still came along to help him.

That particular day, as Nate watched him lift one of the full buckets of thick, warm, frothy milk, something seemed different about his father. It took a minute before he figured out what it was.

"You shaved," Nate said.

"Yup," he said. He was still pouring milk, not looking up.

"Why?"

"I just felt like it. Now and then when I stare into the mirror, I like to remind myself what I look like."

"I think of you more the other way," Nate said. "With a scruffly face."

"I didn't used to be like this, you know," his father said. "I used to be more like you. There was a time, I figured I'd be a professor or something. Get myself a college degree. I would've shaved every single morning, then. Worn a suit and tie and everything."

"I like you being a farmer," Nate said. "If you were a professor, we couldn't come out to the barn together."

They worked side by side for a while in silence. Then his father spoke again. "I was just thinking," he said. "Before long, you know, you'll be shaving yourself."

"I don't need to do that yet," Nate told him. All he had on his cheeks so far was soft, downy fuzz, like his mother's Ultrasuede jacket his grandparents had bought her.

"But you will. It'll happen before you know it."

"Maybe," Nate said. He was afraid his father might want to start talking about the facts of life or body changes.

"I should give you a few pointers, for when the time

comes. There's a right way and a wrong way of shaving."

"I figure you'll show me when I'm ready," Nate said. "It would probably make more sense then."

"Still," his dad said to him, "I might be gone when you get around to it. Off on a trip or something. You know how it goes."

Nate didn't know how it went, actually. His father hardly ever went anyplace, and when he did, Nate went along.

"Anyway," Nate said, "there's not all that much to it, right?"

"Ah," said his father. "That's where you're wrong."

He took a comb out of his pocket then. He held it up to his face, sideways, flat against his cheek, and dragged it across the skin very slowly, as if it were a razor. "Always down, not up," he said. "You need to go with the growth of your beard. Don't fight your own skin.

"There's certain times in a man's life," he told Nate, "that it's important to have a good clean shave."

"When?"

"When you're going out on the town with a woman you really like and you hope to be kissing her," he said. "That's one. I remember when I first met your mother, back when I got the job at Poppa's. I shaved every morning—and evenings, too—just in case the opportunity might come up."

Nate hadn't kissed anybody. It was one of the things that worried him, actually.

"And what's another one?" he asked. "Another situation where you need a shave?"

"When you're going away someplace, and maybe people won't be seeing you for a long time. And you want to leave them with a good impression. You want them to remember you in the best light."

"So why did you shave this morning, Dad?" Nate asked him. "You aren't going away anyplace."

His father just looked at him and ruffled his hair. Then he got up off his milking stool and walked out the barn door. It was the last time Nate saw him, except for that afternoon, when the bloodhounds brought him in.

From where he stood in the hallway now, Nate heard the clatter of dishes. Officer Scruggs setting his coffee cup in its saucer, probably. Nate imagined him reaching for a chocolate or studying his fingernails, the way he always seemed to be doing.

"Your husband was a difficult man to live with, from what I hear," he said. "It wouldn't be all that surprising if you just got fed up with those moods of his. Especially recently, after he'd lost all that money and thrown the family into debt. Terrible pressure with two kids to think about."

Nate's mom didn't reply. Nate hated that about her—that she would just sit there and let the police officer treat her this way.

"I'm asking you to think back again to that morning, Mrs. Chance," Officer Scruggs said. "Maybe you followed your husband out to the field? Let's say the two of you got in an argument. He had the gun with him, maybe, and things got out of hand. It wasn't like you planned it or anything."

"Nothing like that happened."

"So how do you explain the fact that the gun hasn't turned up?" he asked her. "If a guy shoots himself, he sure doesn't hide the gun after."

"I could no more tell you where that gun is than I'll find a million dollars in this cookie jar," she said.

Sixteen

THE FARM WAS SLIPPING AWAY FROM THEM. WITH SAM Carter demanding payment on the loan note, Nate's mother and grandfather were trying to figure out a way to pay it back and still hold on to the place. When he got down out of his truck and came in the house now, Poppa had the air of a person headed to a funeral. Grandma brought food over. Uncle Harold stopped by and told corny jokes that everyone pretended were funny, while Aunt Sal rolled her eyes. Junie wet the bed almost every night. Nate spent all his free time walking their land, looking for the rifle, and working on the cloud chamber.

Mostly it was Nate who got Junie up in the morning, stuffing her damp sheets in the dirty clothes hamper. Their mother had lines above the bridge of her nose all the time, like a pair of parentheses, and even Junie knew not to expect anything of her. Junie'd given up asking her to bring her to Brownie meetings.

These days, even driving to the grocery store was more than their mom could manage, it seemed. When the box of Cocoa Puffs gave out, Nate took to fixing things like toast or fruit cocktail from the pantry or chocolate pudding for breakfast. Sometimes their mother would still be in bed when the bus came, and Junie would call out to her, "Have a good day," like she actually believed it might happen. On the mornings they didn't see her, Junie would leave a draw-ing—of herself, usually, and sometimes of their whole fam-ily, including their dad. *Love, love, love,* she'd write on the bottom.

"Oh, Junie," their mom said once, when she came in the kitchen and found one of the pictures. "I know I've let you and your brother down."

"No, you haven't," Junie said.

Yes, you have, Nate thought, bitterly.

At school Larry and Travis were always together, eating lunch side by side, playing catch out on the field, going off to Larry's house afterward to work on their project. Larry had explained to their science class that the two of them were building a robot that was supposed to put food in your dog's bowl when you told it to, though it was hard for Nate to imagine either one of them getting it right.

Naomi ate lunch with Nate, unwrapping that horrible-looking egg salad sandwich her mother made for her every single day, without variation, accompanied by a handful of celery sticks and a vanilla wafer. If he were still friends with Larry, they'd be discussing the upcoming baseball season, but with Naomi, he talked about the cloud chamber or music. Though Bob Dylan, Joan Baez, and the Beatles were still her favorites, she had discovered a pair of singers called Simon and Garfunkel. And there was another one she really loved—an artist like herself—named Joni Mitchell.

Amazingly, their cloud chamber was starting to look almost exactly like the one in the diagram in *Scientific American.* But they still needed an old watch with a luminous dial to put inside, so they could test if the chamber would reveal the presence of radioactive ions.

Nate's grandfather was over at their house a lot more than he used to be, overseeing what was left of the chores with the half dozen cows that remained, lending a hand loading the milk in the truck to bring over to Meadow Gold. Sometimes Nate would see him looking out to the field behind the house where his father had disappeared.

"Poppa," Nate said one afternoon as the two of them were pouring milk into the separator. "You know that science fair project my friend Naomi and I have been working on? The cloud chamber?"

"Thingamajig out in the implement shed."

"I was wondering if you might have an old watch to give us. One with numbers that glow in the dark."

"That would be my good watch, son," Poppa said. "You think I've got myself a backup?" He'd gotten it years ago. Nate knew that every night when he took it off, he put it back in the original velvet box from the store where he'd bought it.

"I know it's special, Poppa, but we'd take real good care of it. We'd have to take the glass off the front, but we'd put it back after."

"Here's how things were in my day, Nathan," his grandfather told him. "If you had a loaf of bread, you were lucky. If you had a watch, you were a wealthy man. Nobody had time to think about what was happening up in the sky, with stars and what have you. We had crops to plant and cows to milk."

"I know, Poppa," he said. "I was just wondering."

His grandfather stopped pouring milk and looked up at Nate. "These haven't been the easiest times for your sister and you, have they?"

"It's okay."

"Just try to get it back to me in one piece," he said, undoing the buckle. "If a man doesn't know the time of day without a watch on his wrist by my age, I guess he's got a problem, doesn't he?" He handed the watch to Nate.

Nate's mother had stopped playing her piano. At night she sat in the kitchen, sipping tea and talking on the telephone with Aunt Sal. About the only music at their house besides Junie's two 45s was Nate's Beatles album, played on Junie's old kiddie turntable, with its needle that was so old, the voices of John and Paul sounded scratchy and a million miles away.

More and more lately, when he thought about what was going on, it seemed to Nate that the only safe place was just where his father always told him it would be: outside, looking up at the sky. He stood there in the darkness now, studying the constellations, the new moon, and Venus. Beyond that lay whole other galaxies besides their own. A million other suns, each with its own system of planets. A billion stars. Places where nothing that was going on down on earth made a difference. He hoped there was a window in his dad's hospital room in Warm Springs, where he could look out and see the sky. Maybe, if he was looking up right now, he could take some comfort in thinking that the very stars that shone on him were shining on his son, too.

Junie never talked about their father when their mother was around or in front of their grandmother and Poppa. But at night, upstairs, she'd call to Nate to come and lie down next to her and help her get to sleep.

"I miss Daddy," she said one night after he'd read her a chapter of *Beezus and Ramona* that featured the father. One of those regular-type dads, like on TV.

"I know, J," Nate said to her. "I miss him too."

"I don't understand why we don't get to see him. Even if he's sick in the hospital, we could go visit. We'd cheer him up."

"It isn't up to us," Nate told her. "The hospital where Dad's staying is far away from here, and nobody will take us."

"It's not fair," Junie said. "When it's my birthday, I'm going to make Mom take me. If she won't take me, I'm going by myself."

He looked at his sister—her pale face, her thin, wild hair she was always trying to curl. He could remember the day his parents brought her home from the hospital—his father setting her on the bed in her pink blanket and unwrapping her like a present.

"Take a look at what we brought you, Nathan," he'd said. "A perfect baby girl. It'll be your job to look after her."

"How do you propose doing this, Junie?" Nate asked her now. "Seeing as how Warm Springs is hundreds of miles away."

"I'll ask Poppa to take me," she said.

"Oh, right," said Nate. "Even before this happened, Poppa was fed up with Dad, you know that. He's never forgiven Dad for that bad crop of hay. And a million other things."

"But he likes me."

"It doesn't make any difference. You're a kid. He thinks he knows best."

"So what are we going to do, Natie?" she asked him.

It occurred to him, looking at her—looking at her looking back up at him—that she actually believed he could come up with an answer. Seeing that made him feel like he had to. "I don't know yet, Junie. But I'm working on it. I promise, I'll get us to Warm Springs somehow."

They were quiet for a moment, studying a picture of Ramona and her father in the book—a happy, normal pair whose biggest problem was Ramona eating too many apples one time.

"I'm going to sing Daddy my new song when we see him," she said. "You know, 'Yellow Submarine.' And I'll bring him a picture I drew." It was of herself on her horse, Bucky, wearing a cowboy hat and swinging a lariat. "I'll hang it on the wall next to his bed. For him to look at, till he gets to come home."

In Junie's mind, the thing that was going to make everything all better was just getting to see their father again and bringing him home. Nate understood it wasn't that simple. He had never known anyone whose parents got divorced, and the word had not been spoken in their house. But from the way his mother and Aunt Sal and his grandparents acted, he had begun to realize that none of them saw his dad as a part of their lives anymore. It was hard to imagine that they would ever again live as a family, the way they used to.

What he hoped for—that seemed attainable—was to accomplish what old one-armed Frank had suggested: to make his father proud of him in some small way. If he could just lay one huge and glorious victory at his father's feet—in the form of the science fair prize—maybe he could make his dad understand how important he had been to his son.

Every time Nate imagined it, the picture was always the same: He was standing in front of the whole school—the teachers, the kids who talked about him behind his back, Larry. *I owe this award to my dad,* he'd say as he stepped up to the microphone. *He taught me that what's going on down on earth is just a small part of the story. My dad taught me everything I know about life out in the universe.*

He and Naomi would get to attend the state finals then, of course. They'd ride in style, with the science teacher and the other winners—first and second runners-up. *I have to bring my little sister along,* he'd explain. And since he was the winner, who could say no?

It would be nice to win the state championship, too, but that wasn't what mattered most. The important part was getting out to western Montana in a blaze of glory. From there, it wouldn't be hard for him and his sister to make their way to Warm Springs and find their dad, at the end of some dark and lonely corridor, waiting for them.

Seventeen

IT WAS THURSDAY AFTERNOON. NAOMI WASN'T COMING over because her parents were saying she'd gotten behind on her Bible studies. On the bus Larry and Travis weren't sitting together, and Larry was looking mad.

When Nate got off, there were police cars in front of his house again. One of the officers was riding a three-wheeler over the fields where, this time last year, Nate and his father had made the first runs with the tractor. Another man was there with a diving suit and mask, like Lloyd Bridges on *Sea Hunt.*

"What's going on?" Nate asked Poppa, who was out in the implement shed working on a blade.

"That blasted rifle. They're still looking for it. They're bringing in men to dredge the pond."

"They'd better not still be around on Saturday when Junie's party's going on," Nate said. "She's been looking forward to it for weeks."

"I don't know what all the fuss is about a birthday party," Poppa said. "Back in my day we didn't have birthday parties. We worked."

On the bus the next afternoon Junie was bouncing out of her seat. "You know what tomorrow is, huh, Pamela?" she called out to a girl two rows in back of her. "My birthday party! And everyone's invited, remember? Wait till you see my special cake."

"There's going to be games," she told Debbie, the girl who said, every time Junie asked if she could come, that she had to check with her mother.

"And prizes for the winner. And prizes for everyone else, too, so no one feels left out."

"I'm not sure yet if I'll be there," Marsha told her. "My mom thinks we might be busy."

Nate felt his stomach clench and his throat tighten.

"Don't worry if you don't have time to buy a present," Junie told everyone. "There'll be plenty of other presents. Just come."

When they climbed off the bus, Nate was relieved to see the police and the diver gone. They had found nothing in the farm pond, Poppa told him. "Waste of taxpayers' money. What else is new?"

Junie raced ahead of Nate, toward the back door of the house. In the kitchen their mother had set out all the ingredients for baking Junie's cake, just like she'd promised. Junie inspected the packages of food coloring and sprinkles, the different-colored candles, and the letters that spelled out BIRTHDAY GIRL and LUCKY SEVEN. At the bottom of one bag she found a pair of plastic clowns, each holding a bunch of tiny balloons.

"These are even cuter than I was dreaming they'd be," she told her mother. "This is going to be the best birthday ever."

They set to work on a Betty Crocker mix called Strawberry Swirl to make the birthday cake look like a tent, and then Junie added yellow coloring to the store-bought vanilla frosting they'd chosen for the roof. After the cake had cooled and they'd spread on the frosting, her mother let Junie hold the tubes of other colored frosting—green, blue, and purple—to make stripes.

As she squiggled them on, Junie chattered about the games she had planned: Pin the Tail on the Donkey, of course, only they would use a real cow instead—old Muriel, out in the barn, who hardly ever moved. The girls would try to find the spot on her to stick the fake tail, with the winner getting a container of bubble solution and a bubble wand.

"Then Duck Duck Goose, with a bouncy ball for the prize," Junie explained. "Then Musical Chairs, with 'Doe, a Deer' for the music on account of that's Janet's favorite song. Then Grandmother's Trunk, because you don't have to run for that one, which is good for Evelyn." Evelyn had broken her leg skating that winter and was still in a cast.

"And then we'll open the presents. And even if I get something I don't like very much, I'll say I do."

They would celebrate the family birthday tonight, with Grandma and Poppa and Aunt Sal and Uncle Harold.

"Sometimes," Junie reflected, licking the spatula, "kids get a little wound up at parties. Like Debbie, for instance. At her birthday last summer, she had a tantrum after the presents were opened because she didn't get the mosaic tile kit she wanted."

"Debbie always struck me as a little spoiled," their mother said.

"Well, anyway," said Junie, "I've been thinking about that and planning out in my head how to stay calm, so I won't have a tantrum like Debbie."

"I couldn't ever picture you doing something like that. You're such a nice person."

"Even nice people can flip out sometimes, Mom," Junie told her. "It happens."

"Mom," Nate whispered, "I need to talk to you. In private." She was washing the dishes, but now she followed him to the pantry.

"We have to say something to Junie about this party tomorrow," he told her. "I've got a bad feeling that hardly any kids are going to show up."

The look on his mother's face reminded him for a second of his little sister waking up from a nap. "Why would you think that, Nate?" she said. "Who's going to ruin a little girl's birthday party just because our family is having problems?"

"You're not the one who rides the school bus every day. Kids can be mean."

"If a few parents are narrow-minded enough to keep their children from attending Junie's party, they'll have their conscience to deal with," she told him. "But your sister's invited practically half the school to this event of hers. It's just as well if not everyone comes. We might not have enough favors and prizes to go around if they do."

"You don't know what it's like in town, Mom," he said to her. "People are talking about us. Parents are telling their kids not to talk to me. Why do you think you hardly have a single piano student left?"

She didn't answer. Of her five original students, the only one remaining was Buster Haines, the librarian, who had been working on "Für Elise" for the last four years.

"You gotta listen to me, Mom," Nate said. "Junie could get hurt here."

"I know more than you think about what's going on," she said. "But I don't know what you want me to do about it. And even if there was something I could do, to be honest, I don't think I have it in me."

•   •   •

For the family birthday dinner Uncle Harold brought Chinese food: chop suey and fried wontons and chicken fried rice. Poppa had complained that he didn't like foreign cooking, but Nate's mother had told him it was Junie's night.

They gave Junie her presents after supper. From Aunt Sal and Uncle Harold, a dress with puffed sleeves, buttons in the shape of hearts, and a built-in crinoline slip that made the skirt stick out like a princess. "I'll wear this for my party," she said. Their mother gave her a set of day-of-the-week panties and a Skipper doll. Nate's present was a pin in the shape of a kitten. He had picked up a pair of horse barrettes at the five-and-ten that he'd slipped up his sleeve without any problem, but he decided it was bad luck to give his sister a birthday present he hadn't paid for. He had put the barrettes away till he could bring them back to the store.

Their grandparents' present came last: a pink two-wheeler, with streamers and a bell. Poppa had wheeled it in from the porch, and now they all gathered round to admire it.

"I always wanted a two-wheeler," Junie said. "My dad was going to teach me to ride one."

There was silence for a moment then, broken by Uncle Harold. "Never mind," he said. "I will."

Their mother went into the kitchen. When she came out, she had fortune cookies and the root beer floats Junie had asked for, with a candle stuck in the ice-cream part of Junie's. She was singing "Happy Birthday," and everyone joined in. Junie blew out the candle.

"I hope I didn't need to have seven candles to get my wish," she told them.

They were just finishing dessert when the phone rang. Nate's grandmother went to answer it in the kitchen. Nate heard her voice change from her usual friendly tone.

"I don't think that will be possible," she said into the receiver, speaking low. "She's tied up right now."

Things were quiet for a moment. Then Grandma spoke again.

"I don't think it's a good idea," she said, even more hushed. "It would only get her upset."

"Who is it, Mother?" Nate's mom called.

They all knew.

"I said *no*, Carl," his grandmother said. But his mother had gotten up now to take the phone.

"Carl," she said, "I don't want you calling here. You've done enough damage."

"It's too late for that," she said after a pause. "I'm not interested in hearing this."

Their grandmother tried to distract them, asking Junie about her day at school and if her class had sung "Happy

Birthday" to her, but Junie's attention was locked on the telephone in the other room.

"It's my daddy!" Junie said, her voice rising. She got up from her chair so fast, she knocked over her float. "He remembered my birthday," she cried. "Let me talk to him."

Their mother's voice was almost too quiet to hear. "Can't you hear what's happening? You've got her in a state."

"Don't get mad at him," Junie was calling.

In the kitchen their mother's voice grew louder. "The police are acting like I did it, Carl. All on account of you not telling them any different. They dredged the pond yesterday, looking for your gun."

Silence again, except for Junie, who had run to the phone and was tugging on her mother's hand to get hold of the receiver. "Don't, Mom," she said. "Just don't yell at him."

She was pounding on her mother's arm now. "Let me talk," she pleaded. "I need to talk to him." Junie flung herself against her mother, hitting her stomach. Of the two of them, the stronger one appeared to be Junie. At last, her mother handed the phone over, as if the effort required to keep on resisting was just too great.

"Daddy!" Junie wailed into the receiver. "You remembered my birthday!"

Silence. Junie gripped the phone with both hands, like reins on a bucking horse.

"Daddy? I'm here," she yelled into the receiver. As if the problem was that she wasn't loud enough.

They all listened, nobody speaking. From where he was seated, Nate could make out his sister's face, with its look of longing and hopefulness and fear. She stood that way for a minute, whispering, "I love you, Dad. I miss you, Dad. You should come home now," as if she were a spy behind enemy lines. Then nothing.

She handed her mother the receiver. "He must've got sad after you said all those mean things," she said. "He wasn't there."

Again, silence.

"You ruined it," Junie said finally. "I wanted to talk to Daddy. That was my birthday wish, and you spoiled it."

"If somebody spoiled things around here," their grandmother said in a tight voice, "I don't believe it was your mother."

But Junie had left. She was running upstairs. She must have flung herself on the bed, because they could hear the sound of muffled crying and then the familiar opening bars of "Surfer Girl" as her record player clicked on.

Suddenly it was Saturday—party day—and it seemed, to look at Junie, as if she had put from her mind her father's call.

Kids weren't expected until one o'clock, but Junie was up by seven, getting ready. By eight thirty the table had been set.

They didn't have enough chairs for so many kids, so their mom had set out pillows on the living room floor and a buffet in the kitchen with the tent cake and a big bowl of potato chips. Also M&M's and party hats and a giant basket to hold the goodie bags. Junie and Nate had worked all afternoon the day before putting the treats in the goodie bags: a noisemaker, a lollipop, a balloon, and a sticker for every guest.

Junie watched *Cartoon Cavalcade* for a while, but then she gave up. "You know how it feels, Natie," she told her brother, "when you're too excited to even watch a show? That's me."

"I just want you to remember, Junie," Nate said. "Even if some people don't make it, you can still have a good time. Small parties are a lot more fun, actually."

But Junie wasn't listening. She made a sign that said WELCOME FIENDS for their front door and scattered a trail of M&M's from the gravel driveway to the house, in case anyone had a hard time figuring out where to go. She asked Nate if he would put on a different shirt—*The Man from U.N.C.L.E.* one that was her favorite. "I never told you before," she said, "but Debbie Fredricks has a crush on you. So be nice to her, okay?"

He would, he said, explaining that having a seven-year-old think he was cute was not exactly his dream in life.

She wanted to put ribbons on Bucky, but her mother said not to. Bucky was too unreliable to have around a bunch of children, anyway. He could kick. So Junie put ribbons on one of their cats, Snowball, instead, while Nate blew up balloons and taped them to the walls.

At eleven thirty their mom made Junie take a nap, even though she swore she'd never sleep. She lay on the bed, calling out every couple of minutes, "Is it time to get up yet?" until finally their mother gave in and said, "Okay."

By quarter past twelve Junie was dressed and ready, standing by the door. She had picked out her mother's outfit too: a green dress that showed off her red hair, with matching green earrings shaped like four-leaf clovers and high-heeled shoes she hardly ever had any occasion to wear. "You look just like a mom on a TV show," Junie said. "Mrs. Cleaver, maybe, or Donna Reed. But even prettier."

At one o'clock, when the guests were due to arrive, Junie decided to put on a record—the Beach Boys. "Promise me, Natie," she whispered. "You wouldn't ever mention how I sometimes have accidents at night, right?"

"Not in a million years, J," he said. "Anyway, I think you're going to outgrow that, now that you're seven."

At quarter past one Junie was still looking out the window. No cars had pulled up. "Maybe they took a wrong turn," she said. "Maybe they forgot the directions." Nate didn't point out that everyone who rode their bus knew exactly where they lived.

At one thirty, when there were still no guests, Junie sat

down on the sofa. "I don't understand," she said in a quiet voice. "They all knew about my party for ages."

"Maybe some of the kids got sick," Nate lied, knowing as he said it how lame it sounded.

"They didn't want to come," she told him, her voice flat. "They think there's something bad about our family."

"Anyone who'd think something like that is just plain dumb," said Nate, relying on Naomi's theory. "You wouldn't even want to have those people as your friends."

"Yes, I would."

At ten minutes before two they heard the sound of a car on the gravel. For Junie, it was as if an electric shock had shot through her body. "They're here!" she called to Nate, who had gone up to his room by then.

Nate looked out the window. A car had arrived finally: a station wagon, very old. The driver got out first—somebody's mother, definitely. She walked slowly around the side of the car, opened the back door, and leaned inside.

Very slowly, the passenger got out: Lynnette, the girl with cerebral palsy, who sucked on her collar. She was wearing a party dress, and her hair had been curled too tightly, with barrettes put in odd places.

Walking was difficult for Lynnette, particularly when she was excited. Small, happy yelps came out of her as she lurched across the lawn, her head jerking in random-seeming directions, first toward the barn and the cows, then at the sight of the balloons tied to the dogwood bush by the door.

Junie stood in the open door, waiting for her. She stood very straight, with her hands at her sides, and she had a smile on her face, like she'd stood in front of the mirror first and put her fingers in the corners of her mouth and moved her lips around till they got into the right position.

"Hey, Lynnette," Junie called out to her when the girl and her mother got close to the door. "You came to my party! I was waiting for you."

Lynnette's mother started explaining to their mom how difficult it was to get her daughter dressed sometimes. "We still wear diapers for special outings like this," she whispered. "Not that she really needs them anymore. Just to be on the safe side."

Junie took Lynnette's hand then and led her through the mud room to the living room, with all the balloons and the decorations. Lynnette was making some noises that Nate couldn't understand, but Junie evidently did, because she patted Lynnette's hand and put her finger very gently on Lynnette's lips.

"Don't give it away, what my present is," Junie said. "It should be a surprise."

Lynnette had brought Junie two model horses, it turned out. October Sky and Palomino Pal.

"We had some games set up," Junie told her, "but I was thinking: Do you think it might be funner if we just played horses? You could use one of mine."

They sat on the floor, making horse noises, which Lynnette could do almost as well as Junie. Once, when Lynnette got excited, Junie took one of the special circus-theme napkins and dabbed up a little of the saliva that was starting to trickle down Lynnette's chin.

Watching his sister—the tender way she took Lynnette's hand and led her out to the barn—Nate had never felt more love for her.

"I'm just showing Lynnette my pony," Junie called out to her mother as the girls made their way through the mud in their party shoes, holding hands.

When they came back in the house, they sat down at the kitchen table, put on their little clown-style party hats, and had cake and ice cream. Lynnette sang "Happy Birthday," and Junie did too.

That evening, after Lynnette had gone home, their mother put her arms around Junie and held her for a long time. "I'm so sorry," she said.

"It's okay," Junie told her.

Their mother went to bed then, even earlier than usual. Junie folded up the wrapping paper from Lynnette's gift and carried it up to her room to save in her craft box.

When she came back downstairs, Nate had started

wrapping the cake in aluminum foil. Junie stopped him.

"I was thinking," she said. "We don't really need to save the rest. It's never as fun the day after."

Nate dumped the nearly untouched tent cake in the garbage. Then, like a hummingbird to flowers, his sister moved through the dark rooms of their house, pricking the balloons, one by one, till you would never have known there'd been a party at all.

Eighteen

"IF IT MAKES YOU FEEL ANY BETTER," NAOMI TOLD Nate at lunch on Monday, "you're not the only one whose family has problems. My father found the chapter on evolution and Charles Darwin in our science book, and now he's taking me out of class until we're finished with that unit."

Nate didn't understand at first.

"It's in the Bible, silly," she explained. "God made the earth in seven days. Any other idea—like the possibility that we might have come from apes and that for a few million years there might have been dinosaurs walking around— amounts to blasphemy."

"What did you say when he told you?" Nate asked.

"I knew he'd check up on it sooner or later. I'm just hoping nothing's going to get in the way of me being in the science fair with you."

"It's kind of amazing he lets you come over to my house, when you think about it."

"He says it's Christian charity to befriend people who've fallen on hard times. They want me to invite your family over for dinner, in fact. Trying for converts, I bet you."

Mrs. Torvald called to invite them to Sunday dinner the very next day. Because their mother hardly ever answered the phone anymore, it was Nate who took the call. He knew, from all the times he'd heard his mother respond to some invitation to a potluck or something, that he should ask what they could bring.

"Just bring yourselves, Nathan," Mrs. Torvald told him.

The one who was most excited about having dinner with the Torvalds was Junie, of course, who loved making new friends and never felt her family had as lively a social life as she would have liked, particularly not since what she called "my dad's accident." She had not said anything more about her birthday party, though on the bus now, she no longer called out her cheerful greetings to the other kids or offered compliments if one of the girls had a new coat or lunch box.

Hearing they were invited over for a meal at somebody's house—somebody who wasn't a relative—had thrilled his sister. She changed her clothes three times that afternoon, trying to decide on the right look after having been discouraged by Nate from her first choice: a shirt that said I BELIEVE IN BARBIE.

They were due at the Torvalds' at five o'clock. At twenty to, when Nate came downstairs in a clean shirt and chinos, he found his mother in the kitchen, still in the pants she'd been wearing all day as she'd cleaned out the implement shed with Poppa.

"Is that what you're wearing?" Nate asked her.

"Listen, honey," she told him. "I was thinking I'd just let this be a visit for you and your sister. Uncle Harold said he'd pick you up and bring you home. I'm just not feeling up to it tonight."

She was trying to sound casual, but Nate could see her hands shaking. She had reached the point recently where she hardly ever left the house.

"It could be good to get out," he told her, knowing it was a losing battle. The picture came to him—crazily—of families on TV shows he and Junie watched, families that were always having barbecues or doing fun things with their neighbors. Not that an evening with the Torvalds was likely to be as lively as how it was when the neighbors got together on *Dick Van Dyke* and they all rolled up the carpet and started dancing.

"Maybe some other time," Mom said, placing a couple of pieces of silverware in the cutlery drawer, as if in slow motion.

"Yeah, right," Nate said. The bitter, disgusted tone of his voice took even him by surprise.

It was as if he'd punched her. "It's hard for me . . . ," she began, so softly that he could barely hear her.

Something came over him then, like he was in his old Soap Box Derby car, heading down Spengler's Hill with no brakes. He couldn't stop himself.

"You think it isn't hard for the rest of us?" he said. "You think you're the only one with a problem?

"You never do anything," he spat out. "You just mope around all day, leaving it to the rest of us to take care of everything."

He might have thought that seeing her then—her thin frame in the worn shirt, her trembling hands—would make him want to comfort her, but he hated her, for how weak she seemed. The next words came out slow and deadly.

"I can see why my dad couldn't take it anymore."

"I loved your father so much. You aren't the only one around here who's lost him."

"You still have us," Nate yelled. "Did you forget that?"

On the drive over to the Torvalds', Junie did all the talking. She sat on the bench seat in the front next to Uncle Harold, recounting the story in a book her teacher was reading, about a boy in Holland who entered a skating race.

The Torvalds lived in a small ranch-style house just outside of town with a sign over the door that said GOD BLESS THIS HOME. A van was parked out front that Naomi's father used for his missionary work, doing Bible study classes with juvenile delinquents, shut-ins, and unwed mothers.

Heading up their front walk, Nate imagined how he'd explain his mother's absence.

Really sorry my mom couldn't come, see, but the police have been giving her a hard time, acting like she shot my dad . . .

My mom couldn't come because Sam Carter might be repossessing our property, and she's got to make a bunch of calls, to see about selling the cream separator . . .

My mom couldn't come because she can't keep her fork steady anymore when she eats. As for my dad, don't even ask . . .

"My mom had a headache," Nate told Mrs. Torvald when she opened the door. "She said to tell you how sorry she was."

"Sorry to hear that," Mrs. Torvald replied. "I bet a good night's sleep will do the trick."

Naomi was in the kitchen. She was wearing a dress Nate had never seen—her church dress, maybe—and her hair was in a bun. Reverend Torvald sat at the head of the kitchen table, reading, but he got up when Nate and Junie entered. Nate studied his belt, imagined how it would be to feel its slap against his skin. The Reverend extended his hand for Nate to shake.

The food was all set out on the dining room table: a loaf

of Wonder bread and margarine, a bowl of gray-green canned peas and another bowl of potatoes, and a chicken they had somehow managed to cook without the skin turning even slightly brown. It had a color that reminded Nate of Mr. and Mrs. Torvald themselves.

"I never saw a chicken look like that before," said Junie. "Our chickens are crispier."

"That's probably because you buy them at the store in town," said Mrs. Torvald. "These are boiled. We buy them in bulk, at mission surplus. Vacuum-packed, in the can, so all you have to do is heat them up."

"Gerald," Mrs. Torvald said, when they sat down, "will you say grace?"

"Father, we thank you for the blessing of sharing our table on this Sabbath with your children Nathan and June," he said. "Pray for their souls and for the souls of their loved ones. Grant them your forgiveness for whatever offenses they may have committed that they might know the light of your divine and precious love."

They all said, "Amen."

"Why do I need forgiveness?" said Junie. "I didn't do anything bad. I just got here." Her face had taken on a worried expression.

"You were born in sin, June," Reverend Torvald explained to her. "And like all of us, you sin again and again, every day. We are blessed that the heavenly father,

Jesus Christ, our Lord, forgives us all our sins and offers eternal salvation to those who accept him as their savior."

"No matter what I did before?" she asked. "He still forgives me?"

"I'm sure there can't be anything you would have done in your short life that the Lord couldn't forgive," Mrs. Torvald told her.

At the other end of the table Naomi looked anxious to change the subject. "So," she said, "can you believe that Nate has the first hundred and eleven digits of pi memorized?"

"That is certainly some kind of an accomplishment, Nathan," said Reverend Torvald. "Though to be honest, I would rather see a young person such as yourself turn his powers of study to the scriptures. Now, there is a subject worthy of carrying in your mind at all times. That's the only story we need to know."

"Not that our daughter has done so well in this regard," Mrs. Torvald added, looking at Naomi first, then Nate.

"But she's real good at science," said Junie. "Wait till you see the project her and Nate have been working on. The cloud chamber."

Neither of the Torvalds appeared particularly interested in that.

"And what exactly is this project designed to prove or illustrate, if I may ask?" said Reverend Torvald. "Remind me."

Nate considered the question for a moment, trying to assess whether there was anything in the nature of a cloud chamber that could offend Reverend Torvald.

"It's a box that lets you see the pieces of actual stars that blew up jillions of years ago," Junie volunteered. "Once Nate and Naomi's cloud chamber is all set up and we shine the light inside, you get to see the sparkles the star bits make when they travel around in the air."

"We're hoping to win first prize," Nate said. "It should be amazing."

"I suppose we all have our own definition of what is amazing, Nathan," said Reverend Torvald. "To Mrs. Torvald and myself, what's amazing is the light of the heavenly spirit of Jesus Christ, our Lord."

"All Nate meant was, we've been working hard to do a good job, right, Nate?" said Naomi.

The thought came to Nate that watching the flash of light through the cloud chamber—like doing a geometry proof or watching a calf being born—would be, for him, as powerful an indication of a plan and order to the universe as what the Torvalds found in their Bible. "I find God in the night sky," his dad had said one time. Nate did too.

He cut into his chicken. Inside, the meat had the same pasty gray look as it did on the outside. He moved his piece around the plate and reached for a slice of bread instead.

"One time when I was six, I went into my mom's room and took her pin that had a diamond in it, and I brought it to school," Junie said. She was still thinking about unforgivable sins, apparently. Maybe it was being in the presence of a minister that made her feel like confessing all of a sudden.

"I am sure you recognized your error and learned your lesson," Mrs. Torvald said.

"It's just that I always wanted a sparkly pin like that," Junie said. "And there was this girl in my class who was always bragging about her locket. I wanted to show her."

"I'm sure the Lord forgives you, June."

"At least I brought it back, huh? The worst is if you keep it forever."

"I'll tell you two acts of man I believe the Lord considers beyond forgiveness," Reverend Torvald said. "The first is the act of a woman taking the life of her unborn child. The second is a man choosing to take his God-given life by his own hand."

"Like killing himself?" said Junie. "Or trying to?" She had peas on her fork, and it was halfway to her mouth.

"That's right, June," he told her. "Abortion and suicide. Anyone who commits such a crime will burn in hell for all eternity, a fate more terrible than you or I can comprehend. Pray to God we never find out."

Nate studied his sister's face as she sat there. She set her fork down, with the peas still on it. She looked as though a ghost had just walked through the room.

"If I can forgive a person for something like that," she said, "I would've thought God could."

Nineteen

"I HAVE SOMETHING TO DISCUSS WITH YOU TWO," Nate's mother told them over breakfast the next day. For a moment Nate thought she might finally tell them about their father—how he was doing, when he might be getting out of the hospital. But it was about Junie's pony.

"I know you love Bucky, sweetheart," she said, putting a thin arm around her daughter's shoulders. "But it doesn't make any sense to spend money on feed and shelter and shoes for an animal you can't even ride when I can barely come up with money for the electric bill. Not only that. That pony is dangerous. Just today he kicked his hind leg at Rufus. It's a wonder Rufus didn't need stitches. As it was, he only spilled a five-gallon bucket of cream."

Junie and Nate knew where their mother was going with this, of course. Nate studied Junie—the still, slow curtain of sorrow lowering over her features, the anxious tension in her shoulders.

"Your grandfather has talked to a rancher he knows over in Salt Creek," their mother said. "He's willing to take Bucky and put him out to pasture. A lot of people would just send him to the glue factory and get a few dollars for him, but I'm willing to give Bucky away to find him a nice home."

"He has a nice home," Junie said. "With us."

"We can't keep him anymore, Junie. It's just too difficult."

Junie started to cry. "Bucky's my best friend," she sobbed. "He's going to start acting normal soon."

"I'm sorry, honey," their mother said. "I've made up my mind. There's nothing you can do to change it. They're picking Bucky up tomorrow afternoon while you're at school. You can say good-bye to him in the morning."

Normally, Nate woke up a little after six, which gave him just time enough to take a shower, dress, and wolf down a quick breakfast before Henry pulled into the drive. That morning, for some reason, he was wide awake just after five. He put his hand on the glass of the window, same as always, to get an idea of whether it would be a long or short underwear day. Short, definitely.

He looked out to the yard. The snow was almost completely gone, and though the branches on the laurel tree were still bare, it would be just another few weeks until the leaves would be budding. And the birds were back. Just over the clothesline a single brown snipe made its unmistakable swoop skyward, then dove straight down, as if on some kamikaze mission. Nate could hear the faint sound of melted snow running through the creek behind the shed.

He glanced toward the barn. Their remaining cows would be standing inside in their drowsy, stand-up sleep, their udders full and ready for milking. Then he remembered: Off in the far stall Bucky would be munching on his last trough of hay before their grandfather's friend came with his trailer to take him away.

Nate thought about Junie—the look on her face the day their father had brought Bucky home to surprise her; her tears, long after their mother had tucked her in last night. "I want my dad," she had wept when Nate came in to comfort her. "If my dad was here, he'd never let them take Bucky."

Nate recalled his promise to bring Junie to Warm Springs to see their dad. Maybe more than getting his father back for himself, even, Nate wanted his father back for Junie.

That was when he spotted her. At first, in the hazy semi-darkness, he thought it was the Laffertys' old dog, Festus, ambling across the yard, but then he saw it was his sister. She was dressed in her jeans and Keds, the Dale Evans shirt she loved, and the fake chaps Uncle Harold had given her last Christmas. It was too dark to make out the expression on her face, but she had a determined stride, an air of purposefulness.

She pulled open the barn doors. For Nate, that was easy enough, but for Junie, it took several tries, even with both hands and the whole weight of her body pushing. She disappeared into the barn then, and he stood there puzzled, looking out into the early morning quiet.

A few minutes later she emerged carrying Bucky's bridle and reins, which she kept on a hook inside the door. Now she was moving toward the place in the field where her pony stood grazing. She walked very slowly, as if the ground were made of thin ice and one wrong move might cause her to fall through. She knew that a single sudden movement might make the pony bolt.

But Bucky just stood there, even when Junie reached him at the spot inside the paddock where he stood munching on grass. As their father always said, Junie had horse sense like no one else he'd ever known. The way Poppa could study the milk a cow produced or the curve of her belly and know what she needed in her diet or that she'd gotten into clover the week before, Junie knew how to handle a horse.

She leaned her head close to Bucky's and stroked his neck. Nate couldn't make out the words, but he could see her speaking softly into her pony's ear. She stroked his withers and ran her small hand over his side.

Very slowly, she placed the reins in her right hand and threw them gently over Bucky's neck, the bridle in her left hand. Bucky pawed the ground uneasily. She spoke to him again. *Easy, easy,* Nate figured she'd be telling him. *I won't hurt you, boy.*

She had the bridle in her right hand now as she slid the bit in Bucky's mouth. He shook his head vigorously, and for a moment Nate worried Bucky might rear up or even kick his sister. But she reached into her jeans pocket for a carrot, and as she fed it to him the pony even nuzzled Junie with his head.

Junie walked him over till he was standing alongside a large flat stone in the paddock. She stepped up onto the stone, slid her right leg over Bucky's back, grabbed hold of his withers, and pulled herself up till she was seated, bareback. She sat up straight, as if she were a girl in a horse show, in some fancy ring. And before Nate could do anything, she had pulled the reins short in her hands. Crazy as he was, Bucky knew what a clucking sound meant from a rider: *Go.*

Nate knew he needed to act. His sister was doing this brave and crazy thing that a part of him wished he had the courage to attempt himself. He knew he should call her back, tell her no—the way a parent would—but the adventurer in him could only hold his breath and pray the pony wouldn't throw her.

But when he saw them take off, good sense overcame him. He bolted down the stairs two at a time and jumped the last three, then dashed out the door. By the time he reached the yard, Junie and Bucky were on the gravel at an easy trot, and for a second Nate could have kidded himself into thinking that it wasn't so dangerous after all, what his sister was doing. Junie had Bucky under control. It was the thing she'd always wanted: Finally, after all these months, she was getting to ride her pony.

But he also knew Bucky couldn't be trusted. There was no telling when the pony might get spooked.

His mother's Mercury was sitting in the yard. Nate opened the door and turned the key that his mom always left in the ignition. Very slowly, he pulled out onto the gravel driveway, far enough behind his sister that Bucky wouldn't go nuts.

With Junie on his back, Bucky was trotting at a steady, ordered gait. Junie's wispy brown hair blew in the wind. The air felt chilly with the sun just coming up, but it didn't look as though Junie cared. She was heading west, toward the road, toward town.

"Warm Springs," Nate said out loud. "She thinks she's going to see Dad."

That's when it happened. From the opposite direction, the Meadow Gold truck, which hardly ever came by any-more, was heading down their road to pick up the jugs of cream they'd left in the creekside cooling box. At the sight of the truck, Bucky panicked. He jumped the fence, into the field, and took off at a gallop. And then, suddenly, he was not simply running fast, he was out of control, as if his tail were on fire.

"Oh, man," Nate said. He could see Junie leaning against Bucky's withers with her whole body, trying to get a better grip. He imagined how hard her heart must be pounding. She was pulling on the reins, but the motion had no effect. Bucky was running like a horse that knows the glue factory has his number.

Nate pulled himself up tall in the driver's seat, gripped the steering wheel, and put his foot to the floor. A person had to be careful on dirt roads like this one not to let a vehicle skid out and spin, or even flip, his father had told him: "You'll want to brake on a curve, but that's exactly what you shouldn't do. To maintain control, keep your foot on the accelerator."

Even though Nate couldn't see his sister's face, he was near enough to register—from how she held herself on the pony, her legs wrapped tight against his midsection and her hands clutching handfuls of mane—the full scope of her terror. "I'm coming, Junie!" he yelled into the wind. Still flooring the gas pedal, he watched the speedometer climb to thirty-five, then forty miles per hour.

When he got close to the field where Bucky was—galloping and lurching wildly, snorting and shaking his head—Nate brought the car to a halt and jumped out. He vaulted the fence and ran across the field till he was up in front of Junie, with Bucky flying toward him headed for the line of wooden fencing that separated Nate's family's farm from the big, wide-open section of land that was his grandfather's ranch. At the far end of the fence lay an open gate, so there was nothing stopping Bucky from flying straight through. And once he did, Nate knew, there would be no opportunity to hold him back, with a thousand acres of open fields beyond. His sister would be halfway to Wyoming before Nate could catch up with her.

Unless he could get to the gate and get it shut before Bucky reached it.

Nate shot across the field like Mickey Mantle rounding third. In his whole life he never ran so fast, but he made it, moments before the pony did, and slammed the gate. When Bucky got there, he reared up and turned in a wild, confused half circle, snorting and whinnying. Junie held on for dear life and called out, "Whoa, boy."

But the field beyond the fence still beckoned Bucky. Nate could see his sister trying to control the pony by shortening the reins in one hand and turning him, but Bucky was past controlling. He was disoriented, cockeyed, crazy, and where the wooden fencing had momentarily stopped him, Nate realized suddenly that the barbed-wire fence along the far end of the property would not. And that's exactly where Bucky was heading. A horse doesn't register barbed wire, their father had told them. Nate knew that, and Junie did too. He imagined Bucky crashing into it, the wire tearing into his skin, his legs buckling. And Junie, falling—on her head, or even crushed beneath her pony's weight.

Only one thing left to do. Nate positioned himself squarely in front of the barbed wire as Bucky came at him. Like a bullfighter, he cut off Bucky's movements—first alongside one stretch of wire, then alongside another. If he could just get Bucky to move in the direction of the barn, he knew what would happen. The pony would want to go home again. He'd want the safe, familiar territory where food and water and his own warm stall were waiting.

At first Bucky only seemed confused and frantic. Then, just as Nate had been hoping, the pony began to lose steam. He shook his head, and Nate could see the look change in his eyes. He took one final unsteady step toward the fence, stopped, and then turned 180 degrees in the other direction. Back where he came from. Back to the barn.

Nate jumped in the car and pulled the door shut. He drove as fast as he could toward the barn without the risk of setting Bucky off again. Reaching the paddock just as Junie and Bucky did, he leaped out and ran up in front of the exhausted pony. Sweat dripped from the pony's glistening haunches and midsection.

"Bring him up, J," he called to Junie. "Rein him in now."

He saw her pulling with the full force of her small body, so hard she was leaning back as far as she'd been leaning forward before. The pony let out one last whinny and skidded to a sideways stop. Nate ran to catch up with them.

"Junie," he cried. "Are you all right?"

She was gasping for breath, unable to speak. Bucky was panting too, his coat as wet as if he'd traveled through a rainstorm. Junie still clung, trembling, to his back, her head against Bucky's sweat-drenched mane. His big, wide chest was heaving, and his nostrils were flared. One hoof pawed the ground. His head shook. Like his rider, he trembled.

"Let's get you down," Nate said quietly to his sister. He held his arms out and let her slide into them. He could feel her heart pounding in her small, narrow chest as she fell against him, sobbing.

"We were going to go to Warm Springs," she said when she had breath enough to speak. "We were going to see Daddy."

"I know," Nate replied.

Twenty

THAT AFTERNOON WHILE THEY WERE AT SCHOOL, THEIR grandfather's friend came and took Bucky away. As soon as she got home, Junie walked out to the barn, alone, and stayed there a long time. When Nate came in her room later, she was sitting on the bed. The picture she'd made of herself riding Bucky had been taken down off the wall. He saw it, crinkled in a wad, in her wastebasket.

"I know you're sad, Junie," their mother told her later at dinner. "Maybe someday we'll get you a horse. One you can really ride. Bucky has a lot of problems, that's all."

"Just because someone's got a few problems doesn't mean you should give up on them," Junie said, moving her fork around her potatoes.

In the old days, Junie would spend most afternoons out in the barn with Bucky, except for every other Tuesday, when the Brownies got together at the legion hall in town. But now, with her pony gone and her mom not wanting to drive anywhere, Junie mostly watched television—game shows or the reruns of family situation comedies like *Father Knows Best* and *Leave it to Beaver.* One of her favorites was *My Three Sons,* about a man whose wife wasn't around who raised three boys with the help of a crusty old geezer named Uncle Charlie. It bothered Junie that they never talked about what had happened to the mom on the show. Nobody ever acted sad that she wasn't around. Junie had looked hard, she told Nate, but it didn't seem like they had a picture of her on their wall, not even in the dad's bedroom.

"If it was our mom and she died or something, I'd want to have a picture to remind me," she said one day as they watched the show together.

Nate didn't comment, but he knew what she was thinking. Over the weekend their mother had taken down all the photographs that had their dad in them, including the one in the front hall from their wedding day.

Helping Junie get ready for school this morning, Nate had found a little stash of photographs—three snapshots she must've taken out of the family album and hidden in her sock drawer. One showed their dad as a very young man, skinny as a beanpole in his baseball uniform. In another, taken at a fair someplace, their dad and mom were standing behind cardboard cutouts of a cowboy and a cowgirl, with just their faces showing through holes. They were grinning at each other. The last picture showed Dad, Mom, and Nate in front of the Mercury when it was new. Mom was holding a baby—Junie—wrapped in a blanket. Dad stood beside her, with one hand on the hood of the car and his other arm draped proudly around her shoulder.

Nate had studied the pictures carefully. He knew, to look at the last one, that his parents had been in love then—as clearly as he knew that they weren't anymore. He figured it made his sister feel better, knowing things had been different once, so he'd put the pictures back in Junie's drawer.

Studying his little sister now, as she sat curled in her spot on the couch—her eyes locked on the happy-looking family on the TV screen, her forehead with its worried frown—Nate tried to think of something that might cheer her.

"Hey, J," he said. "Suppose we could get Uncle Harold or Aunt Sal to take us into town Friday night, you and me. Maybe we could go bowling."

Junie's face brightened. The bowling alley was pretty run-down—four lanes, with a pinsetter that broke so often, you never knew if you'd get to finish your turn. But if she couldn't be on a horse, bowling was her next favorite thing.

"How 'bout we get Naomi to come too?" she said. Junie liked Naomi, who didn't ignore her the way most older kids did.

"I guess I could ask her," Nate said. "She probably can't come, though."

• • •

Surprisingly, Naomi said yes, and Uncle Harold said he'd pick them up and drop them at the lanes, then bring them all home afterward. "My treat," he told Nate, giving him a five-dollar bill.

Junie wore orange corduroy pedal pushers to the bowling alley and her cowgirl vest with a flowered shirt underneath. "Don't you wish we could get to wear these in real life?" she said, lacing up her multi-colored bowling shoes.

"Actually, no," Nate said, tying his.

But Naomi, on the bench between them, thought that would be great too. This was her first time bowling, she told them. "I always wanted to go. But my family never does this kind of stuff."

"Don't worry," Junie said. "I'll show you the ropes."

They were just setting up the scoring—Junie first, then Nate, then Naomi—when they heard a cascade of giggles near the door. Looking up, Nate saw Pauline Calhoun and a group of kids from his class, including Larry, Travis, and Jennifer, collecting their shoes and score sheets. His stomach turned over.

Pauline and the others settled themselves on the bench by the lane directly beside theirs. Nate tried to keep his eyes focused straight ahead.

"Oh boy, oh boy," Junie said as she picked up her first ball. "I hope I get a strike."

She planted herself at the line and bent down, with the ball in both hands, as if she were launching a baby duck in a pond. Very gently, she released it.

The ball wobbled slowly down the lane as Junie stood, watching its progress. Partway down, it rolled into the gutter.

"Oh, too bad," Naomi said. "I thought that was going to be a great shot."

Nate looked at the two of them and shook his head very slightly. No way he could pretend he didn't know them.

"That's the hard thing about bowling, Naomi," Junie explained. "You can have the best aim in the world, and still sometimes, for no reason, the ball just wiggles in some bad direction."

Nate might have disputed this, but what was the point? One lane over he heard the crash of falling pins—a strike for Larry.

On Junie's second try she knocked down a single pin. She jumped up happily. "One! I got one!" she cried.

Nate got up to take his turn—a spare. Junie and Naomi went to the bathroom. When they got back, she reported that Pauline and her friend had been there too. "You should see her bracelet," Junie whispered to Nate. "It's got all these jingly little charms. A heart and a puppy and even a bicycle with a wheel that really moves. She took it off when she was washing her hands, and I got to look at it."

"Great," Nate said, though he was familiar with

Pauline's bracelet and how, for every special occasion in her life, her father gave her some new charm.

Then it was Naomi's turn. Unlike Junie, she started from farther back and took several steps, bringing the ball forward from behind her back, to gain momentum. But she had started on the wrong foot, and her motion was off balance. The ball, by the time she released it, zigzagged wildly before ending up, like Junie's, in the gutter. Same with her next ball.

"Don't worry, Naomi," Junie said kindly as Naomi sat down. "There's lots of time to catch up. Nate and me've been bowling lots longer than you, so don't feel bad."

The game felt endless to Nate, all the more so because of the fun the others seemed to be having in the next lane. Normally, he was a good bowler, but he was getting low scores tonight, sixes and sevens mostly. He got up to buy a bag of candy for the three of them. When he returned, Pauline was standing in front of Naomi, hands on her hips.

"Okay," she said. "I know you have it. Give it back."

"I don't know what you're talking about," Naomi said. Her hair was gathered up in a series of irregularly spaced pigtails—another one of Junie's hairdos for her, held in place with barrettes in the shape of kittens and yellow plastic happy faces.

"My bracelet," Pauline said. Jennifer came over to join her. The two of them looked witheringly at Naomi—her mismatched clothes, her dumb-looking hair.

"We know you took it in the bathroom. Give it back."

"I never took anything," Naomi said. "I don't steal."

"I'll have you know those charms are sterling silver," Pauline said. "When my dad finds out, he'll have a cow, and it'll all be your fault."

"I never touched your dumb bracelet," Naomi said again. Next to her, Junie placed a hand on Naomi's arm.

"She never touched your dumb bracelet," Junie repeated. "Why don't you go mind your own beeswax?"

"Just because you don't have anything pretty of your own doesn't give you the right to take nice things from someone else," Pauline hissed. "Just because your own clothes are always so gross . . ."

Larry and the others had stopped their game by now.

"She told you already, she doesn't know anything about it," Nate said. "We're trying to play our game here."

But it was ruined after that. They finished up their game, but no one suggested they start another one. The final scores were Nate, 86; Junie, 9; Naomi, 4. They brought their shoes back, paid, and left, calling Uncle Harold from the pay phone outside to come pick them up.

"Done so soon?" he asked. "We figured you'd be there another hour or two, at least."

"It wasn't so much fun after all," Junie said when he got there a little later. "Bowling's not as great as I remembered."

Twenty-One

JUNIE'S FIRST-GRADE CLASS WAS PUTTING ON A PLAY, *The Three Little Pigs.* Once, Junie would have been excited to have such a good part—the little pig who builds her house out of bricks. But she had barely mentioned to Nate and their mother that the performance was coming up. She hadn't even asked them to rehearse her lines with her. And when Nate asked her about it, she'd said, "It doesn't matter if I get my lines wrong. My teacher's going to be sitting right there with the book if anyone forgets."

"What's got into you, Junie?" Nate asked after school, as he sat at the kitchen table having a glass of milk.

For a minute, she didn't say anything. She was drawing in ink on the belly of Palomino Pal. Just a small mark, almost like a cattle brand. Still, Nate never would have thought she'd do something like that to one of her precious model horses.

"You lied to me," she said at last.

"What are you talking about?" Nate asked her. "When?"

"You promised we'd go see my dad. I waited. You never did anything." She was scribbling fiercely now. Black lines, back and forth, on the horse's flank.

"I keep thinking about him sitting in a room someplace all alone," Junie said to him. "I keep thinking how he's waiting for us and he's wondering why we never come."

"He knows it's hard," Nate said quietly. "He knows we love him."

"But we're not there, are we? If you love somebody and they're in trouble, you should be there. And you promised you'd take me."

He didn't make excuses. Junie was right. She had trusted him. He'd said he'd take care of it, and he hadn't. He was no better than Aunt Sal, who'd said to him all those weeks back, "Be patient." And then did nothing.

"I wasn't going to tell you until I was sure," he said. "I didn't want you counting on this, but I do have a plan. The thing is, it depends on the cloud chamber."

Junie stopped drawing on the horse. She looked at him hard. "Your science fair project?"

"The winner at our school gets a trip to the state finals. They're in Butte. Near Warm Springs."

"What about me?"

"You get to bring a family member along. Most people bring their mom or dad, but I'll take you instead."

Junie didn't ask what their mom would say when she found out. Or how he knew for sure he'd win in the first place. She trusted him to work it out, was all. She set her horse down and threw her arms around her brother. She ruffled up his hair the way she said made him look like Ringo.

"You are the best brother in the world," she told him. "I knew you'd figure something out."

"It's still two weeks to the science fair," he said. "Not to mention, there's no guarantee Naomi and I can win."

"I know you will."

Nate was washing up in the boys' room at school when he saw it: a crude drawing, scrawled in Magic Marker on the wall above the paper towel dispenser. The picture showed a stick-figure man, with a downturned mouth and crazy hair, lying facedown on the ground. The exaggeratedly curvy figure of a woman was standing over him, a gun pointed at his head. And next to them were the words *Chance's Farm: Cows and Nuts.*

Underneath, in a different-colored marker, someone else had already contributed another picture of a similar stick-figure man sitting behind bars, with his arms tied around his body like he was wearing a straitjacket. *Nate Chance's dad is a psycho,* it said. There was a third drawing too: this one of Naomi, obviously, but with a bandana over the lower half of her face and the words *Wanted:*

Jewelry Thief. Someone had scribbled next to it *Stole Pauline Calhoun's charm bracelet!*

Nate pulled down a towel and dried his hands. He wet the towel some more and ran it over the marker, but the words and images didn't go away. He would have crossed them out, only he didn't have a marker himself. He went back to class.

Fourth period was gym. "I'm sure I don't need to remind you boys that Little League tryouts are this Saturday," Mr. Johnson told them. "We're counting on you all to show up."

Last year, Nate had pitched. He wasn't always the starter, but by the end of the season the coach had said he had the most reliable arm in the league. "We're going to be facing some pretty tough competition from over in Leopold next season," he'd told Nate after their final game. "But if you keep developing your curveball and get a little more accuracy, we're going to give those boys a run for their money."

So that had been the plan. Nights back during baseball season, when he and his dad drove home from the field together after games, they would talk about the pitches Nate had thrown, going through the at bats of every single player on the opposing team. His dad had been a pitcher too, and even after the injury that had messed up his leg, he could still throw a great curveball and slider. For a while they'd worked together on Nate's pitching every day.

After his father slipped into his black hole last fall, he hardly ever caught for Nate anymore. But Nate still carried the bucket of balls out back every afternoon, all through October and November, aiming for the red circle of a target on the mattress they'd hung against the barn. More and more, he was hitting it too. When he went to Larry's, the two of them played catch for hours, and when he was home and throwing on his own, Junie would come out with him and settle herself on an old tractor seat mounted on a tree stump their dad had made. When the bucket of balls was empty, she'd scurry to collect the balls. And after Nate was done throwing a second round, he'd play catch with her, the way their father had done with him in better days. Sometimes he'd try out his screwball, but he could never get the motion right.

Nate would never have believed the day would come when he'd pass up baseball tryouts. But now he pictured how it would be to see Larry, hanging out on the bench with the other guys, and he thought about the words on the bathroom wall at school.

"You coming out for pitcher this year, Chance?" Mr. Johnson asked him in gym class.

"I don't know," Nate replied. "I'm pretty busy these days getting ready for the science fair."

"Try to make it," he said. "The team could use you."

Nate stopped in the boys' room again after school. He was in a stall with the door closed when he heard familiar voices at the sink.

"Hey, get a load of this," Travis was saying. "Someone drew a picture of Nate Chance's wacko father and his mom that blew him away. Pretty funny. I bet Pete did it."

"People shouldn't put up stuff like that," Larry's voice said. "It's not Nate's fault, what happened. How'd you feel if it was you?"

"Jeezum," said Travis. "When did you turn into the pope? It's just a goof, is all."

"That's probably not how Nate sees it," said Larry.

Hearing his old friend's voice just outside the door, Nate couldn't move.

"All I can say is, I sure hope he's not crazy enough to show up for tryouts on Saturday," said Travis. "Nobody wants a psycho kid on our team."

Nate heard the sound of someone pulling a towel from the dispenser and then the door swinging shut. He waited a moment, to be sure, then stepped out.

He caught a glimpse of his face in the mirror, and the sight startled him. Over the last stretch of long, dark weeks, his features seemed to have changed. He looked stronger than before, and older.

It was funny, he thought, the way Travis's words were affecting him. He'd planned on skipping the tryouts. He and Naomi were going to run their test on the cloud chamber on Saturday morning, now that the long-awaited package of dry ice had arrived.

But hearing Travis's words had changed that. Nate figured Naomi would understand if he put their science fair work off till later that afternoon so he could go to the ball field first. There was no way he was going to miss those tryouts.

Twenty-Two

NATE WAS THROWING BASEBALLS AT THE MATTRESS when Officer Scruggs pulled up. "My mom's in town," he called out.

He didn't add what she was doing there: trying to hold off Sam Carter, who was on the verge of foreclosing on their farm.

"I didn't come to see your mother," the policeman said. "Actually, it's you and your sister I was looking for. I thought we could have a talk."

"What about?" Nate hurled the ball at the strike zone. He was off by a mile.

"Why don't you come sit in the patrol car with me?" Officer Scruggs said. "Have a chat. You want a stick of gum?"

"No thanks."

"I may be an old guy," Officer Scruggs said, "but I still remember how my folks could drive me crazy sometimes, growing up. My mom in particular. Not that I didn't love her to death, of course. But you know how it is with mothers."

"Not really."

They got into the car. The motor was running, to keep the heat on, and from the radio came the scratchy voice of the dispatcher, talking about a detour on Route 46 and someone's pig on the loose out by the old Turner place.

"I know you love your mom, Nathan," the officer started out. "And you wouldn't want to tell us anything that you'd think might get her in trouble. You might even feel like you have to keep certain things secret from me."

"I don't have any secrets," Nate said. "My mom doesn't have anything to hide."

"Still, it would be understandable, given what your dad was going through, if your mother felt frustrated and impatient sometimes. Anyone could understand that. Anyone could lose their temper at a person now and then."

"I guess," Nate said. "I wouldn't know."

"Your dad sounds like a very interesting and unusual individual," Officer Scruggs went on. "But no doubt, it wasn't always easy living with him. I bet even you got a little put out with his ways once in a while yourself."

"No."

Officer Scruggs looked frustrated. He flipped through his notes, as if he was trying to think of what a detective on TV might say.

"According to your hired man here, your parents argued on occasion. That would be accurate, am I right?"

"Not much," Nate said. "Nothing big."

"I understand your mother slapped your father. According to one source, she was heard to say she hated him."

"My mother doesn't hate my dad," he told Officer Scruggs. "And she doesn't hit."

"I understand your father lost a lot of money on a bad crop. No doubt that made your mother upset. Maybe your parents argued about that? Maybe your father threatened your mother, and she might have felt a need to take down the gun, just to defend herself?"

"Nothing like that happened."

The police officer wasn't quitting. "Okay, then," he said. "I have to ask you about the morning of the shooting, Nathan. Would you say there was anything unusual about your mother's behavior that day?"

"No."

"Would you say your mother was agitated? By that I mean was she upset?" He said it like Nate wouldn't know what "agitated" meant.

"She was normal," he said. "If anyone was acting a little different, it was my dad. He wanted to say all these things to me, like instructions for shaving. Like he might not be around or something."

It felt reassuring, having something to say about that day that was real. Like Cassiopeia, the constellation that you can always locate, that helps you get your bearings for the rest.

Officer Scruggs looked like he didn't know what to say next. "But you can't deny your mother was upset with your father?"

The guy had definitely been watching too many episodes of *Perry Mason.* But even though he was trying to act like a big-shot lawyer, Nate knew he was really nothing more than a small-town policeman who spent his whole life giving talks about bicycle safety at schools and rounding up lost pigs.

"I don't remember that," Nate said.

"Come on now, son," the officer said, impatience creeping into his voice. "We've got a witness prepared to testify that your mother told your dad she wished he was dead."

Rufus, Nate thought.

Nate took a deep breath and turned in his seat so he was facing the policeman. "I'll tell you one more time," he said. "My dad was feeling real bad all winter and for a long time before that, too. He told my sister and me we'd be better off without him. In the barn that morning he kind of said he might not be around in the future. All my mom ever did was try to keep things together for my sister and me."

It was strange, hearing himself say these words. He knew this wasn't what the policeman wanted to hear. The man didn't even write it down in his notebook. But as much as he loved his father and as angry as he'd been at his mother, Nate couldn't let Officer Scruggs believe his mom could have shot his dad.

"Okay," Officer Scruggs said. "That's probably enough for now. I'll be wanting to talk with your sister next."

Nate felt a wave of anger pass over him as he thought of his sister sitting in the car with Officer Scruggs. The policeman would have gum for Junie too, of course, and she would take it. If Officer Scruggs asked his sister if their mom had a bad temper, Junie might think about the times she'd left her model horses lying around on the living room floor and say, *She gets real mad sometimes.* If he asked, *Did your mom ever get angry at your dad?* she'd tell him, *Lots of times.* And he would write it all down in his notebook and bring it back to the police station.

"So," Officer Scruggs said, "if you'd just go get your sister for me . . ."

Nate drew in his breath. He imagined he was standing on the pitcher's mound, with a full count and the best hitter in the league coming up to bat. He gave the officer a look meant to bore straight into his eyeballs. He wound up for the pitch and released it. A rocket.

"My sister's only seven. You have no right to make her do this, and I'm not going to let you." His voice hadn't actually changed yet, but it sounded deeper than he'd expected.

"Okay," the policeman said. "I'll leave it for now. You can go."

Nate let out his breath. For the first time he could

remember, he had told a grown-up what to do—not just any grown-up, either, but a police officer—and that person had actually done it. He opened the car door slowly and stepped out. Then he leaned back inside and spoke to the man one more time.

"Leave our family alone now," Nate said. "Go away, please."

He closed the door behind him.

Twenty-Three

IT WAS AFTER SUPPERTIME WHEN NATE'S MOTHER finally got home. Nate had gone ahead and fixed Junie and himself a meal: scrambled eggs, popcorn, and Oreos. Junie was in the tub with her horses, and Nate was washing the dishes. He knew as soon as he looked at his mother—her face drawn, hat tipped slightly to one side—that the meeting with Sam Carter hadn't gone well.

"He won't budge on calling in the loan," she said. "We have to sell the farm."

She had mentioned this possibility before, but it had never seemed real. Pictures began to swirl in Nate's head like a sad old slide show—all the familiar spots he'd never thought about much, because he figured they'd be there forever. There was the root cellar where, on long winter days, he and his sister used to make monsters out of old sprouted potatoes; the creek where they sailed their home-made paper boats when the spring rains came; the hayloft

195

in the barn where he and Junie had their Tarzan swing set up; the clubhouse he and Larry had built and the pond where he and Larry had fished. And, of course, there was the land itself—four hundred acres. He'd driven over every square foot of them in the old John Deere.

"Maybe Poppa can help," Nate said, but his mother was already shaking her head.

"Your grandfather's already helped as much as he possibly can. And if the police keep acting like I'm a murderer, he might have to hire an expensive big-city lawyer for me too."

Mom kicked her shoes off and leaned wearily against a kitchen chair. "It's that rifle. They keep coming back to how they can't find the rifle and how that must mean I shot your dad and threw it away someplace."

"They can't send you to jail."

"I wish I could say for sure you were right, honey."

It took Nate by surprise when she came over and put her arms around him—how thin she had become. "I wanted so badly to keep things normal for you and your sister," she whispered.

"I don't even know what normal is," he said.

Saturday morning Junie stayed in her pajamas and watched *Cartoon Cavalcade* while their mother sat at the kitchen table with their grandfather, going over the books again and doing a tool and equipment inventory. Nate had offered to help, but he was relieved when his mother told him, "Never mind, Poppa and I can handle this."

He pushed thoughts about moving out of his head and watched the clock instead. The baseball tryouts were due to start at noon. He put on his cleats, grabbed his glove, and thought about last summer, before the hailstorm, when hopes were high. From the drawer where he kept his baseball cards, he took out his favorite—Sandy Koufax—and stuck it in his pants pocket.

Yesterday he'd decided to ask his mom to drive him over to the playing field for tryouts, but seeing the tight, worried expression on her face, it seemed impossible.

Nate figured he'd warm up a little first out by the barn. Maybe he'd call up Jed Landry and see if he was driving to town anytime soon.

The day was mild at last—the long-awaited scent of spring in the air. Over by the chicken pen Rufus looked up briefly and muttered something Nate couldn't hear.

"You talking to me?" Nate asked, releasing his first pitch, a beauty.

"I take my hat off to you," he said. "Going out for baseball, especially when you don't even know where you'll be living in a few months. I don't reckon I could be that big of a guy, out there in front of all them people, knowing they'd be talking about me."

"That's their problem," Nate said, setting his mouth into a hard line.

"Like I said, I take my hat off to you. Some people, if they heard the talk in town, would lie low. You're more like your pa, I guess. Do whatever darn well pleases you, and to heck with what's happening and what folks say."

Nate faced his mattress target and tried to concentrate. He threw another pitch, imagining it was Rufus's face in the center of the strike zone. Bingo.

"I figured you were going to tryouts, on account of my brother was headed to the field this morning too," Rufus continued. "Our dad's been working out with him ever since the beginning of March, practicing fly balls. Too bad your dad wasn't around to do that with you, huh?"

Nate threw another pitch. Pathetic.

"I may or may not make it to tryouts. What with the science fair and all, I'm pretty busy."

"Oh, right," Rufus said. "You and your girlfriend there."

Nate started to correct him, then stopped himself. What made it Rufus's business to know about Naomi? He threw another ball in the direction of the red circle. It landed in the dirt.

"Don't worry," Rufus said, looking at the ground where the ball landed. "There's worse things in life than getting laughed at, huh?" And he let out a high, thin laugh as he sauntered off.

• • •

For another hour, Nate went back and forth, picturing himself on the pitcher's mound one minute, and the laughing face of Rufus the next. While the minutes ticked away, he saw his father, poised to catch, as the two of them practiced the screwball last summer. He saw Larry and Travis, out on the field without him, laughing over some joke. Maybe about him. He thought about how, that first spring he was old enough for Little League, he'd slept with his glove under the pillow, breathing in the smell of its new leather. He loved baseball, but some of what he loved was being part of a team. Most of all he'd loved that his dad was always there to cheer him on.

At a quarter to twelve Nate took off his cleats. He got out a comic book he'd read a bunch of times before, lay down on the living room couch, and tried to concentrate. In a little while, he figured, he'd call up Naomi and see if she was ready to come over so they could test their cloud chamber with the dry ice. Maybe if he thought about the science fair, he'd get his mind off the tryouts.

Junie came in. "What are you doing here, Natie?" she asked. "Aren't you supposed to be down at the ballfield?"

"I'm not playing this year, J," he told her. "It just feels too complicated. I don't think the kids want me on their team anyway."

His little sister looked at him hard. "So? Who says they're the boss of you?"

"They all talk about our family. You know what I mean."

"I figured out it's easier for kids to talk about you when you're not around," she said. "That's why I decided to be in the play at school—just so they won't talk so much."

"I'd probably mess up anyway," he told her. "Plus, I don't have a way of getting there. The chain on my bike is so rusty, I'd never make it."

"You can take mine."

Nate looked into his sister's eyes. He thought about how brave she'd been that morning when Bucky ran off with her. He wanted to be brave now too.

Her bike was small for him, of course, not to mention pink, with colored streamers and a bell with the face of Barbie on the front. Not exactly the best way to get him the long five miles to town. But that was the least of his problems. He laced his cleats back on and he was out the door. He hopped on Junie's bike and started pedaling full speed.

The tryouts had been going on a good hour by the time Nate arrived at the field. He rode right up to the spot where the players had assembled and lowered the kickstand of Junie's bike, remembering how he'd felt the other day in the patrol car with Officer Scruggs, telling him to leave his sister alone. He shot a look toward the row of boys on the bench

like the one he'd given the police officer. Nobody said anything about the bike.

"I'm glad to see you made it, Chance," Coach Jennings
said to him. "I've been wanting to take a look at that arm
of yours.

"Evans." He pointed to Travis. "I understand you're trying out for pitcher this year."

"I've been throwing to Larry lately," Travis told the coach.
"I've got some pretty good heat on the ball." He got up from
the bench. Nate might have been imagining, but it seemed
like Travis sneered at him as he headed out to the mound.

At first the pitches Travis threw looked inconsistent—
two balls to start it off, followed by a slow curve that even
a bad hitter like Corey Tomkins had no trouble connecting
with. Followed by two strikes in a row. Then another ball.
Another easy hit. Another strike. It went like that for the
first few players in the lineup, though by the end of his try-
out Travis was starting to look impressive.

"You showed me some nice work out there," the coach
said as Travis made his way back to the bench.

Then it was Nate's turn.

He got the feeling, as he stepped onto the pitcher's
mound, that all eyes were on him—not only the coach
and the players, but the mothers who'd come to watch,
and a bunch of fathers, too, and the guy at the hot dog
wagon who had set up shop for the start of the season.

A wave of dizziness came over Nate. He looked down to the dirt, trying to remember how he used to do this. The ball, in his hand, suddenly felt like a foreign object, something that dropped down from space, that he'd just happened to pick up. He tried to remember his father's instructions for putting his fingers across the stitching, imagined how it would be if his dad were sitting there on the bench now, watching. He took a deep breath and pulled his arm back for the windup.

"Sometimes your worst enemy is your own brain," Dad had said to him once. "You let the wrong thought come into your mind at the wrong moment, and suddenly you're lost."

It happened now, the split second before he released the ball—the picture of his father. Not his father as he'd been when the two of them were out behind the barn, throwing pitches at the mattress. The picture that came to him was of his dad as he'd been that day the bloodhounds brought him in from the field—stumbling to the ambulance, blood pouring down his face.

It was too late. He'd let the ball out of his grasp. He'd thrown a terrible pitch, wild to the left. It was so bad, people didn't even laugh, they groaned.

Steady now, he heard his father telling him. *Take your time with the next one.*

In his head he recited the first ten digits of pi, then the ten after that. He pulled his arm back. He looked across the plate, into the eyes of the batter, a boy named Terry Peters who had called him "Psycho boy" in social studies. He released the ball. Fast and true, a rocket into the strike zone, unhittable.

Terry looked surprised. Nate threw him another. Just as deadly.

He mowed down four batters in a row. Then Kirk got a single off him, followed by a couple of pop-ups. But then Nate was back throwing darts, smooth and steady. *Whiff, whiff, whiff, you're out.*

"I've got one more batter for you, Chance," the coach called out. "Kowalski, take a whack at him."

Larry, the best hitter in the league last season, stepped up to the plate. Their eyes met. Nate thought of the first time they'd played together, the summer after second grade—the long hours they had pitched and hit to each other and, afterward, up on his bed, putting together imaginary teams of all their favorite players with their baseball cards. He saw the face of Sandy Koufax lying on the bedspread. And then a different picture: the package of Topps cards he'd pocketed at the five-and-ten the week before. Not even opened.

He wound up. Looked out at his old friend one more time. Fired.

A ball.

"Try him again, Chance," Coach Jennings yelled.

This time he fired a fastball over the plate. Larry swung

and missed it. A look came over Larry's face—not anger or disgust, like Terry. Respect.

Another throw, this one a curveball. Larry caught the side of it, but only enough to foul.

Another pitch. The one Nate and his father had been working on last summer: the screwball.

Larry looked startled. The ball seemed to shoot straight for the center of the plate, then broke sharply to the left, sweeping out of range as Larry's bat kissed air. He swung and missed. *Out.*

There was an audible gasp from the small crowd of parents on the sidelines. Larry shook his head as he walked back to the bench, but more in a good-natured way than mad.

One last kid came up to bat against Nate—another strikeout. As Nate headed in from the mound, the coach patted him on the back. "Looks like we found ourselves a starting pitcher," he said.

On his way home, standing up over the candy-striped seat of his sister's bicycle, Nate passed the five-and-ten store. He slowed down on the bike and, for a second, considered stopping to see what cards they had. But then he thought better of it and pedaled home.

Twenty-Four

AFTER HE'D GOTTEN CLEANED UP THAT AFTERNOON, Nate called Naomi. Her voice on the other end of the phone sounded a little less animated than usual.

"I was wondering what happened to you," she said. "I decided you must be too busy playing baseball."

"The season doesn't start till after the science fair," he said. "Anyway, our project's still the most important thing. Did you think I'd lost interest just because I'm playing ball?"

"I thought maybe once you were on the team, you'd be back with your old friends," she said. "I wasn't sure you'd still want to hang around with me."

More graffiti had shown up on the boys' room wall. Some of it was about his family, same as before. But there was also a new picture of Naomi, with exaggeratedly frizzy hair and a big nose, her overlarge glasses, and her two giant book bags, with papers spilling out of them.

"Listen, just because I'm playing on the team doesn't make me Mr. Popular around here all of a sudden," Nate said. He realized, after he said it, that it wasn't the point, really. He shouldn't be her friend only because he had no other options. She deserved his friendship, even if the others did start being nice to him again. And anyway, he liked her.

"We'll always be friends," he said to her. "Did you forget that we're going to Butte together?"

They had been keeping the precious package of dry ice in a Styrofoam cooler in the barn, wrapped in newspaper, in preparation for the test run of their cloud chamber. Nate lifted the block out very carefully, wearing gloves like the package said, and carried it out to the implement shed, with Junie skipping alongside. He'd told her she could watch them run their experiment if she promised not to get in the way.

As Nate unwrapped the dry ice, a thin mist like steam, only cold, began to rise around it. Naomi lay a towel on top. They lifted the cloud chamber off the workbench and set it, very gently, on top of the towel. "Whatever you do, don't drop it," Junie reminded them.

Once the cloud chamber was in place, Naomi unfastened the box's seal and lifted off the glass top. Nate measured a capful of ethyl alcohol and sprinkled it on the blotting paper they'd attached to the lid. In the center he placed his grandfather's watch face, with the glass taken off to expose the radioactive paint on the dial.

They set the glass top back over the chamber and sealed it tightly.

"What happens now?" said Junie. She was practically dancing, she was so excited.

"Now we wait," Nate said.

They had read, over and over, what was supposed to happen: The dry ice, working in conjunction with the alcohol, would produce an atmosphere of swirling gases. But reading it in the "Amateur Scientist" column was different from actually seeing it.

Nate told Junie to turn on Uncle Harold's projector that they'd positioned so the light would shine right in.

"This is going to be so great," Junie said in a low, husky voice.

"Don't get your hopes up yet, J," Nate told her. "It might not work."

"You got to think positive, you guys."

"I'm just being realistic. Things are always a lot more likely to go wrong than right."

In a few minutes the gases began to swirl as the atmosphere inside the chamber cooled. "Light, Junie," Nate said to her. She shot the beam into the cloud chamber.

"This is when we're supposed to see the ionizing radiation from the watch," Nate said.

Five minutes passed. Nothing. Two more, and still no sign of radioactive particles shooting across. Nate took out their troubleshooting list.

"It says to be on the lookout for air leaks," he read. "Also, there could be a problem with the size of our box. It might be too short or too tall."

Then it started: first just one small streak, then more tiny, spidery tracks of light. Sharp, sputtering flashes zapped through the swirling mist along the base of the chamber. What they had caused to take place seemed like magic, except Nate knew it wasn't magic at all; it was science.

"It's so beautiful, Nate," Junie cried as the mist from the ethyl alcohol gradually evaporated and the rays ceased to be visible.

"I can't believe it actually worked," Naomi added. "I kept thinking a couple of kids would never be able to pull off something this amazing."

"But we haven't reached our goal yet," Nate reminded her. "So far, all we've actually seen is evidence of radiation from Poppa's watch face. The real magic comes if we can spot radiation from star particles."

He lifted the top from the cloud chamber and removed the watch face. Then he dripped more ethyl alcohol on the blotting paper and replaced the lid again. He set the cloud chamber back on the dry ice to cool a second time.

"Now we wait to see the real thing," he said. "Evidence of actual radiation from activity in space."

Once again, the chamber gradually filled with vapors. Junie shone the projector beam inside. They waited. Ten minutes. Fifteen.

"I don't know what the problem is," Nate said. "But we can't leave our dry ice out any longer or it'll melt too much, and we won't have enough for later."

"I bet we just need to leave it longer," Naomi said as he placed the dry ice back in the cooler. "When we do it at the science fair, we'll give it lots more time. And anyway, we've got the rays from the watch as our backup. No matter what, that's pretty impressive."

"Wait till they hear about this at school," said Junie. "Just let them try to make fun of you now. I'm telling everyone on the bus."

"Not yet," Nate told her. "I want people to think we're just doing some dinky little report on stars or something. It's better if we take them by surprise on the day of the science fair."

"And then you'll win," Junie whispered. "And you'll take me to the championships." She didn't have to say the other part. They both knew it.

Then they'd see their dad.

Twenty-Five

IT WAS THE NIGHT OF JUNIE'S PLAY, *THE THREE LITTLE Pigs.* After the show Poppa took everyone, including Uncle Harold and Aunt Sal, out to dinner to celebrate Junie's performance as the little pig who built her house out of bricks. "I'm so proud to be the mother of the smartest little pig," Mom said. Nate could tell she was trying hard to look carefree and happy, but it wasn't as successful a performance as his sister's had been.

The restaurant featured an all-you-can-eat salad bar, with a long counter covered with platters of roast beef, fried chicken, lasagna. Junie was too excited from the performance to eat, but she was walking around to tables that were empty, collecting paper parasols and plastic cocktail swords customers had left behind. Nate had gotten up for seconds.

When he returned, the conversation had shifted from Junie's school play, but for once, the adults didn't cut off their remarks in mid-sentence. Maybe things had finally got so bad that nobody saw the point in trying to conceal them anymore. Maybe they were just too weary to try.

"The police brought in some big investigator from the city yesterday," his mom said, moving spinach around on her plate. "They're still stuck on that missing rifle."

"Your fingerprints aren't anywhere on that gun, right, Helen?" said Aunt Sal. "I bet in all the years you never even touched it."

"That's true enough," Nate's mother told her. "For all the good it does me, if they can't even find the gun."

"The crazy thing is, I can't figure out how the thing could disappear like that," Uncle Harold said.

"What about . . . you know . . . ," Aunt Sal said, making a sign with her head, as if the children wouldn't understand that she was asking about their father. "Isn't he ever going to say something about what happened?"

Junie had returned to the table now, a bouquet of tiny pastel-colored paper parasols clutched in her hand. "Can you believe people just threw these away?" she said.

"I guess," Mom said, signaling with her eyes to end the conversation as quickly as possible, "I guess they just can't pull him back from outer space to remember."

It was Saturday morning. Nate and Naomi were up in his room, working on their poster, when his mother called up to him. "You've got a visitor, son," she said.

Nate heard footsteps on the stairs. Then there was Larry standing at the door to his room. "I know you're probably busy with your project," he said. "But I had to talk to you."

Nate and Naomi were stretched out on the floor with her set of Magic Markers scattered around them. "Be my guest," Nate said. "We're getting pretty close to finishing up this thing anyway." He was trying to sound casual, but his heart was beating fast. From Junie's record player, the Beatles were singing "I'm Only Sleeping."

"Great album, huh?" said Larry. "My sister has it."

"So how's your project coming?" Nate asked him. Larry had still been standing just a few inches inside the doorway, but now he walked in and sat down on the bed.

"Disaster. Travis is a total screwup. He kept saying he had this uncle who was going to show us how to build the robot, but when the guy finally came, all he had was this little model kit from a toy store. Then it turned out Travis copied his whole half of our report on robotics out of the encyclopedia, and Mrs. Unger found out and gave us a zero."

"Too bad," Nate said. "It could have been a neat project."

They sat in silence for a while—Naomi drawing, Nate picking fluff off the rug. "I wanted to apologize," Larry said.

"What for?" Nate said, though of course he knew.

"I acted like a jerk. Didn't just act like a jerk. Was one."

"It doesn't matter."

"My parents," Larry said. "Everyone was saying to stay

away from your family, like it was something we could catch."

"I know," Nate told him. "My sister invited thirty kids to her birthday party. Only one came."

Larry didn't say anything, just looked around the room. The old familiar stuff: the star chart, the Chicago Cubs pennant, the poster of Alfred E. Neuman. The girl lying on the floor with the crazy hair and the uncapped marker in her hand—that part was new.

"You know Naomi," Nate said.

"Hey," Larry said.

"You should see her artwork," Nate told him. "She does these cartoons, as good as *Mad* magazine practically."

They sat there like that. Naomi chewed her fingernail. Nate ran a hand through his hair.

"You rode over on your bike, huh?" Nate finally asked Larry.

"Yup."

"Mine's all messed up. I busted the chain on those jumps we were doing last fall."

"I remember."

"That was my sister's bike I had at tryouts Saturday."

"I kind of figured," Larry said. "Your arm was looking good. I'm glad you're on the team."

From downstairs, they heard Nate's mother calling. "You kids want hot chocolate or something?"

"You guys probably have work to do," Larry told them. "I just thought I'd stop over. It's ages since I've been out here."

"Come by again sometime," Nate said.

"Hey, you ever dig up that old time capsule you and your dad buried that time?" Larry asked him. "I always thought about how cool it was, you two burying all that stuff."

Nate hadn't thought about the time capsule for a while. It had been years since he'd even been out to the animal graveyard, where he and his dad had buried it. That spot by the poplar trees had been his dad's favorite place on the whole farm.

Thinking about how much his father loved it, how seldom anybody thought to go there, a thought came to Nate: The animal burial ground was one place he hadn't gone looking for the gun.

"We should go out there sometime," Larry said.

"How about now?" Nate said.

In five minutes they had their jackets on, and the three of them were making their way across the field. Though the snow had melted, the ground was still damp. The air was clear enough that they could see all the way to the Crazy Mountains along the horizon. Closer by, Nate studied the outline of the Landrys' barn, a stand of cattle grazing on the nearby quarter, and the silhouette of the old green metal windmill his mom was always telling him to stay away from rising into the sky like a lone sentry.

"I've read about people burying time capsules," Naomi said. "I just never actually knew someone who did it."

"You had to know Nate's dad," Larry explained. "He's just so crazy." Unlike most people who'd been making that observation lately, he didn't say it in a mean way. There was admiration in his voice.

Nate knew every inch of their farm, but walking the land now, aware that his family would be leaving soon, made everything seem newly precious—the song of the meadowlarks, the angle of the sun against the barn, the sweet smell of cow manure. He hated the sight of the rich soil lying fallow this way, with no new seed planted for the coming summer. Before, he'd always marked time by the growing season: cleaning and oiling the tractor, then bringing it out of the barn for the first spring plowing; putting in the seed and watching as the field slowly greened up; running the combine over their tall, golden fields and watching the grain shower down from the auger into the hopper at harvesttime; then making the runs to the elevator and the anxious moments of waiting for the final tally—how many bushels, how many dollars.

"I heard my parents talking a couple nights back," Larry said. "My dad was saying how he ran into Bud Scruggs, down at Legion Hall. Even though my dad was the one who said I shouldn't hang out with you anymore, he said it made him feel bad listening to the guy talk about your family the way he was."

"When I grow up," Naomi said, "I'm never living in a place like this. I'm moving someplace where people don't get all huffy just because you're a little different."

"You'd better move to Mars, then," said Larry.

They had come to the windbreak of Russian olive and poplar, the place where the tractor marks stopped. The three of them stepped more gingerly now, past the rusting remains of an old tractor body and a circle of stones that had served, long ago, as the spot where Nate and his father built their campfires. Off to one side, partly concealed in scrub, lay the skeleton of a cow, so perfectly in place, it could have served as the illustration in some animal husbandry anatomy textbook.

"I saw a painting in a library book one time by this famous artist named Georgia O'Keeffe," Naomi said, studying a piece of bone bleached by the sun. "She paints things like cow skulls all the time, in a way that makes you see how beautiful they are. I wish I could bring one of these bones home, so I could draw it, but my mom would kill me."

Nate looked around, hoping to see the rifle. He remembered his dad telling him how this was really the prettiest spot on their whole four hundred acres, and for the first time he could see what he'd meant. Where the rest of their land stretched almost perfectly flat all the way to the horizon, here was this one little rise, marked by the poplar trees. Just next to one of them was the stone they'd set down to remind them of the place they'd buried their time capsule seven years ago. He knelt down and brushed his hand through last summer's dry grass. He touched something hard and cold.

"I found the marker," Nate told his friends.

"You should be the one to dig it up," Larry said, handing Nate the shovel they'd brought.

He plunged the blade into the muddy ground and began to dig. The hole was almost a foot deep when he finally hit metal.

"It's like a real treasure hunt," Naomi said. "Like finding the Dead Sea Scrolls or something."

"Not quite," Nate told her, lifting out the gray metal box and placing it on the muddy ground. "Still, a lot has happened since we buried this thing." Naomi handed him her bandana to wipe the dirt off. He unfastened the clasp on the box.

Inside was a newspaper clipping from the *Missoulian*, with a picture of one of the Russian Sputnik satellites lifting off into space, a plume of flame behind it. The date was 1960. Three months before Nate's seventh birthday.

There was a Sweetgrass County Pioneers baseball cap, his father's team from school days, with a note pinned to the brim: *For my son, Nathan. Future pitching star.* There was a Mounds wrapper with a bit of coconut and chocolate still smeared on the inside. There was a small blue plastic cowboy—that would have been Nate's contribution—and a penny dated 1959. A baseball card—Roger Maris, outfield, New York Yankees, 1960. A piece of paper with a series of numbers on it so long, it covered the page—pi. A seed packet labeled FORGET-ME-NOT and, inside, a lock of red hair.

At the bottom of the box there was a stack of old newspaper comics, and lying on the top was an envelope marked in his dad's firm hand: *To whom it may concern . . . and chances are this means you, Nate!*

Nate showed the envelope to his friends, then very slowly opened it and started reading the letter inside:

It's Monday afternoon, March 21st, 1960, and you and I are sitting here, digesting a chocolate bar, waiting for the eclipse. Any day now, there's going to be a baby born in our family, and you'll be a big brother. I know you'll be a great one.

Someday, when you read this, I hope you know how proud and happy you make me. There might be other things that don't always go the way I hoped they would in life, but one thing that has never disappointed me is you.

Just so you're clear on this: I love you and your mother a whole big bunch. I hope I can do right by the two of you and whoever it is we haven't met yet that's on the way. I may not be the world's most reliable guy, and I don't blame your mom faulting me for it. But one thing's for sure. There's nothing in the world I want more than to see you have a big, interesting life for yourself. The possibilities are endless. Don't you forget it.

Got to go now, almost time for the eclipse. Catch you when you grow up!

Love,

Dad

At the bottom of the letter his dad had drawn an arrow, with the words *Turn this over.*

Nate had to compose himself for a second. He didn't want Larry and Naomi to see him with tears in his eyes. He read what was written on the back.

P.S. So now I want you to look under the pile of newspapers. There's a present in here for you. I'm figuring you're getting up into those crazy teenage years, when your curiosity gets the better of you and you dig this up. So I tried to think of what I would have wanted most when I was that age. Other than a 1942 DeSoto, that is.

Nate dug down to the bottom of the box. His hand felt a package, compact but with weight to it. Even before the paper was all the way off, he knew what his present was: binoculars. Ever since he could remember, his dad used to say how important it was to own a good pair. "A person gets a whole other perspective on life, looking through those lenses," he always said. "Get yourself a good pair of binoculars, and you can see forever."

"That's so cool," Larry said, taking a look through the binoculars. "You can see birds up close and trees in the distance and clouds and everything. I bet if we took these binocs to Wrigley Field someday, we could see the stitching on Adolfo Phillips's glove, way out in center field."

"I just got an idea," Nate said. He pointed to the old windmill just beyond the boundary of their land. "Suppose we climbed up to the top. If that rifle is lying on the ground someplace, and we're looking down with these binoculars, we might just spot it."

Judging by the sun's position, they figured it must be past noon by now, and Nate knew Naomi was supposed to attend Bible study, but she didn't seem to care. With the metal time capsule box under Nate's arm, they headed farther out across the field.

Ever since he was little, Nate had been fascinated by the windmill—the way it rose up out of nowhere on a treeless expanse of flat land. Once the Landrys had used the windmill to run an irrigation pump, but that was a long time ago.

"The county should take that thing down before some crazy kid breaks his neck trying to climb it," Nate's mom used to remark.

As for Nate, he'd never been tempted. Even climbing up onto the rafters inside their barn gave him an odd, queasy feeling. And that was nowhere near as high as the windmill, tall as an apartment building.

No one said anything as the three of them made their way toward the windmill, the new binoculars hanging around Nate's neck.

Then they reached it, the rusty green metal base of the structure planted firmly in the soil, with only flat land and air all around. Up along one side, a narrow metal ladder rose so steep and high, Nate had to lean his head all the way back just to see the tiny platform at the top.

Nate and Larry just stood there, looking up. They had done many scary things in their fourteen years of life, but neither one of them was having an easy time contemplating this one.

"I got to admit, I'm not that good with heights," Larry said quietly.

"Me neither," Nate said. "They give me the heebie-jeebies, actually."

"I want to back you up on this one, man," Larry said. "I just need a little time to think."

"Me too." The sick feeling in Nate's stomach was worse now. He thought he might throw up.

"You know what, you two?" Naomi said. "Heights don't bother me one bit. Back in Maine we had this elm tree that went up forever. One time when I was eight or nine, I made it all the way to the top."

"I don't know," Nate said. "It seems like if anyone's going to risk their neck climbing this thing, it should be me."

Naomi reached for the binoculars and hung the strap over her neck. "Besides," she said, "if I spot your dad's rifle, I'll need you two to go where I point you and bring it in."

She tied her hair back in a ponytail, so it wouldn't get in her way climbing.

She was wearing jeans and sneakers, luckily, but she had no gloves, and the metal of the ladder was cold. Hand over hand, she pulled herself up its rungs while Nate and Larry stood below, coaching her. When she got to the first break, they called up to her, "Way to go, Naomi." She didn't stop but kept on climbing.

Somewhere around the halfway point she hesitated for a moment and looked down.

"You okay?" Nate yelled.

"I was just feeling a little light-headed," she called wn to him. "But I'm fine. I don't think I'll try looking n anymore, though."

Below, Nate watched the figure of Naomi move slowly up the ladder. She was getting smaller now—no more than a dark smudge against the sky.

"How're you doing?" he called out.

Her voice came back to them as if from a cloud. "Okay. But it's pretty windy up here."

"You scared?"

"A little."

She had almost made it to the top when they saw her hesitate. She had paused on a single rung, going nowhere, within a few feet from the walkway that marked the top.

"What do you think's going on?" Larry asked Nate. The two of them were afraid to call up to her, in case the sound of their voices might spook her.

"I can't tell. This was a dumb idea. We shouldn't have let her do it."

Neither one of them moved, watching her. Finally Nate called up, "Are you okay, Naomi?"

Her voice seemed small, coming back to them. "There's a dead bird on the platform," she called, sounding shaky. "With feathers and everything. I can see its one eye staring at me."

"Pretend it's those cow bones," Nate called back. "Just get off that rung."

They watched her slowly raise her right hand to the final rung, her right leg following. She pulled her body up—left hand, left leg. She was at the top. From down below, Larry and Nate let out a cheer. "You did it!"

"I don't believe this," she called out to them, standing straight up on the top platform. "I can see forever." She raised the binoculars to her eyes and scanned the horizon. For a long minute Nate and Larry just stood on the ground, gazing up at her as she surveyed the landscape.

"See anything?" Larry called.

"Not yet."

She moved to a corner of the platform. She turned her body to the right, then to the left, then to the right again.

"She's up too high," Nate said. "From where she's standing, my dad's rifle would probably look like a toothpick."

"I don't know," Larry said. "Those seem like really good binoculars."

They waited. Not a sound from the top of the tower. Then all of a sudden, a shout from Naomi. "I think I see something. It's a glint of light, hitting something metal, maybe. I can't tell what."

"Where?" Larry yelled.

"I need to come down and show you," she called back. She moved cautiously back onto the ladder, with the binoculars around her neck again. Nate couldn't bear to watch as she began lowering herself down. He imagined what would happen if she placed her foot wrong, even once. He thought of her in the cafeteria line, the awkward, unsteady way she navigated with her tray, the orange rolling off that time. He wanted to yell, *Careful!* but no sound came out.

"I can't believe that girl," Larry said. "She's so cool."

"I know," Nate replied.

Then Naomi was on the ground again, making her way toward them with that goofy, loping run of hers, ponytail bouncing. "I think I know where it is!" she cried. "Come on."

She grabbed Nate's hand and took off running, with Larry following behind. They ran to a place near the far edge of the property.

Nate looked around. Nothing. "Over by that piece of fencing," Naomi said. "That's where I saw it."

He walked another twenty yards, surveying each foot of ground as he went. "It's not here."

But just then Larry called out. "Look! She's right."

All this time Nate had dreamed of the moment he'd find his father's rifle. But now that they'd spotted it, he just stood there, frozen.

"Jeezum," said Larry. "What do we do now?"

"The important thing is not getting our fingerprints on it," Naomi said.

Nate couldn't touch it anyway. Looking at the old rifle, which had sat in the gun rack for as long as he could remember, Nate felt sick to his core.

Evidently, Larry was having a hard time too, because in the end, it was Naomi who took off her jacket and, with her fingers inside the sleeves, picked the rifle up.

"Be careful with that thing," Nate said. "Chances are it's still loaded." He still had his batting glove in the pocket of his jeans. Putting it on, he signaled to Naomi to put the gun back down on the ground. Then he knelt beside the rifle and emptied the remaining shells.

Larry carried the rifle to the house while Nate held on to the shells. Walking back, he didn't try to hide his tears. Naomi put her arm around him for a second, then let it hang free again.

"I bet things'll start to get better now," she said.

Twenty-Six

NATE'S GRANDFATHER CALLED THE POLICE TO SAY they'd located the rifle, and a little later, a cruiser pulled up to the house to pick it up. The police report, after they'd dusted for fingerprints, revealed that his mother's were nowhere to be found.

"I'm sorry about what you went through, Mrs. Chance," Officer Scruggs said when he stopped by the house a few days later to give her the news. "I'm sure you can appreciate that as officers of the law, approaching a felony offense of assault with a deadly weapon, we have to consider every possibility. But I'm happy to report, you are now free of further suspicion in the shooting of your husband, which appears to have been self-inflicted."

One thing didn't change. Sam Carter was still foreclosing on their farm. An auction had been announced to sell off most of what the Chance family owned. All that week—the final days before the science fair—Nate and Junie would come home from school to find their grandfather clearing out the barn, oiling the tractor, even—like it mattered now. Their mother moved through the rooms of their house like a sleepwalker, packing belongings into boxes or sometimes just looking out the window.

On Wednesday, Aunt Sal took Nate's mom to Billings to help her look for an apartment. She filled out applications for secretarial positions and took a typing test. "Maybe after I get my feet on the ground, I can find some piano students again," she told Aunt Sal. "Someplace new, where nobody knows us."

Thinking about moving was too much for Nate to take in. If he started counting up the losses, he wouldn't know where to begin, so he tried to stay focused on the science fair instead.

He and Naomi knew that the cloud chamber worked from their dry runs with Poppa's watch face. But so far, the only flashes of alpha and beta and gamma rays they had picked up came from the watch and not, as they'd hoped, from actual radiation star particles they might witness after the watch was removed. The write-up in *Scientific American* had specified that this radiation might be tricky to detect, but they were still trying.

Then there was the written report—Nate's least favorite part of the job. Naomi was supposed to be finishing that up, along with the illustrated poster. But Naomi hadn't shown up at school on the Monday or Tuesday after the discovery of his father's rifle. When Nate called her house Tuesday night, Mrs. Torvald said Naomi wasn't up to talking.

Wednesday night—after another day's absence from school—Naomi called him. He knew the second he heard her voice that something was wrong.

"My parents found out that I climbed the windmill," she said. "It was pretty bad."

No mystery how her parents had found out. The news about Nate locating his father's rifle had traveled all over town. It hadn't been difficult for the Torvalds to piece together the rest.

"My parents said you and I've gotten too close or something like that," she told him. "Like they couldn't imagine a boy and a girl just being friends, without some kind of weirdness going on. And I guess it made them nuts, thinking about me in the middle of nowhere with a couple of boys. So now I'm not supposed to see you anymore."

"That can't happen," Nate told her. "We have to do something." Then, after a moment, "What about the science fair?"

"I guess I won't be going to Butte after all. They don't even want me at the fair at school."

"We worked so hard," he said. "How can they do this?"

"You can do it on your own. If the cloud chamber wins, maybe Larry can go to the state finals with you."

"But you're my partner. You're the one who's earned it."

"I have to go," she said. "I'm not supposed to use the phone."

"Take care of yourself, huh?"

"You too."

When Nate came home from school on Thursday, he found his mom packing her good china into boxes, and she looked tired. Not just tired—bone-weary.

"I know it's a bad time for you, Mom," Nate said. "But I was wondering if you could give me a little help on my science project. I really need you." Saying this, he realized how long it had been since he and his mother had done anything together and how much he missed her. "If not," he said after a second, "I can get Larry."

She set down the soup tureen she had been wrapping in newspaper. "Of course I'll help. I can't think of one thing I'd rather do."

After fixing them both a mug of hot chocolate, she pulled up a chair alongside Nate. He took out the note cards and the library books he and Naomi had been using for their research, and spread the draft pages of their written report, with their dozens of cross-outs and footnotes, across the yellow kitchen table. His mother brought over her typewriter.

"At least there's one thing I'm still good for," she said. "I can type like the wind."

They worked all the rest of that afternoon and into the evening. When they were partway done, Junie came into the kitchen, wanting something to eat. Mom fixed them all sandwiches and set hers down next to the typewriter, so she could keep on working.

All those years Nate had always done school projects with his dad. It had never occurred to him that his mother might be interested. Now she was asking him a million questions, wanting to understand the difference between alpha and beta particles and why it was important to cool the air inside the cloud chamber to just the right temperature.

At eight o'clock they were still hard at work, though his mother took a break to put Junie to bed. "In my day, they didn't encourage girls to think much about science," she told him when she returned to the table with a fresh cup of coffee. "When your father used to talk about things like galaxies and stars, I just figured it was beyond me."

Nate stopped what he was doing and looked at her. "You and Dad are really different types of people," he said. He had hesitated over the words—whether to say "are" or "were"—but he wasn't going to talk about his father as if he were dead.

"That's true."

"So why did you get together, anyway?" Nate asked her. He was afraid that if he said too much, the moment would end. But he couldn't let the chance go by without trying to find out some of the answers he'd been waiting for all this time.

His mom took her fingers off the typewriter keys, and for a second he thought she might get up and walk away. But instead, she said, "We were young, for starters. We didn't know much about what it took for two people to make a life together. But I was crazy about him too. I loved all the wild ideas he used to come up with—exploring caves and building kites and having picnics off in the country.

"That first winter we were together, your father built an iceboat," she told him. "When we put on our skates and took that thing out on the pond, it was like we were flying. He was more fun than anyone I'd ever met."

"How did things get so messed up?"

"The world gets in the way, honey," she told him. "You're trying to support a family, you've got all these responsibilities . . . it just gets so much more complicated. There isn't a whole lot of time left for stargazing anymore."

"Other people's parents have responsibilities too," Nate said. "They don't shoot themselves." He drew in his breath and waited, not sure what his mom would do, but she just sat there like she was thinking hard about what to say next.

"Some people are just sturdier than others. Like your grandpa. Whatever happened to him—even if a fire wiped out this whole place and everyone in it—I can't picture that man caving in. He's one of those people who march on, no matter what. Someone like your dad doesn't have as firm a grip on things. He takes things so hard."

"We should have done more to make him feel better," Nate said softly. "We should have helped him."

"It's one thing to rescue a person when they're in the middle of a lake and they can't swim," she said. "But rescuing someone from what's going on in their own head, that's a lot harder."

Another time, he would have said something to her about how unfair it had been for her and all the other adults to leave him and his sister in the dark the way they had. But he knew his mom was doing what she thought was right, so he decided to leave it alone for once. He figured he and his sister would get to Butte without her help, and that was probably the best way to do it.

He was grateful for this little moment that had passed between the two of them—the fleeting experience of hearing what she really felt. Like a flashing ray, shooting through the swirling atmosphere of a cloud chamber, lighting up for a second, and then leaving you in darkness again. Only at least now you knew: Just because something was invisible most of the time didn't mean it wasn't there.

Twenty-Seven

FRIDAY NIGHT BEFORE THE SCIENCE FAIR JUNIE CAME into Nate's room. He had heard her singing along with "Mrs. Brown, You've Got a Lovely Daughter," and he figured she'd fallen asleep when the singing stopped. But she was wide awake.

"I'm worried about something," she said. "What if there's still no star particles at your school? What if we beam the light in the cloud chamber and all we see is the swirling gases?"

Junie didn't fully understand the difference between sparks from the watch face and the real thing, but she understood it was an important distinction.

"Star particles are everywhere," Nate explained. "There's no such thing as a place that doesn't have any. Plus, I saved our biggest hunk of dry ice for tomorrow, bigger than we used when we were trying it out in the shed."

The truth was, Nate had been troubled about not picking

up real star particles too, but seeing Junie's anxiousness, he downplayed it. "And anyway, it's not the end of the world if we don't get to see star particles. We'll still have the sparks from the watch face to show the judges. That's like our insurance policy."

"So you're going to win, for sure?" she said. "Because I already have my outfit all planned for when we go to Butte."

"Nobody can say for sure what's going to happen tomorrow," he told her. "But I wouldn't worry too much."

Even though he didn't want to say so to Junie, Nate had seen the other projects at school, and to him, it seemed clear: Nobody's was half as cool as the cloud chamber.

On Saturday, Nate woke to rain—and to Junie bouncing on his bed. She had put on "Good Day Sunshine" from *Revolver,* and she was wearing her cowboy boots and the dress with the built-in petticoat that she'd worn for her birthday party. She'd even made pin curls with bobby pins in her hair.

"Hurry, you better get dressed," she told Nate. "We only have a couple hours till the judging starts."

It was a good thing they had the science fair to think about. Otherwise, they'd be spending all their time being sad about their house.

The day before, after Nate had finished his poster and his

report was completely typed, he had gone out to the barn and climbed up to his favorite spot, the hayloft. The last of the cattle had been hauled away in the morning. The sweet smell of hay and manure still hung in the air, but the silence was all new. He'd always thought of the barn as a quiet place—somewhere he could go to think, where the sound of his father's whistling carried like birdsong on the breeze. But with Sophia and Gert, their two last milkers, gone, he realized that there had always been a music to the barn: the sound of cattle breathing and snorting; the slap of their tails against the sides of the stalls; the stomp of a foot now and then; and the wonderful, soothing lowing sound they made—nothing like *moo,* really.

There was no question anymore. They were moving. Mom was almost done packing up the items they were going to keep, for storage in Poppa and Grandma's barn until she found a new place to live in Billings. Everything else was going to be sold at the auction, to pay back Sam Carter. Once their place was sold, the plan was for Nate and Junie to stay at Aunt Sal and Uncle Harold's until school got out. Then they'd join their mother. Come September, he and Junie would be going to a new school, where they wouldn't know a soul.

Nate wondered if his dad knew what was going on. Of course, it was his dad's fault this was happening in the first place. If he'd stuck around and taken care of things, like other people's dads, this never would have happened. If he'd been someone like Poppa, they might not have a lot, but they'd still have cattle in the barn and a tractor, and they'd be sowing seed for the new crop instead of looking out, as Nate did now, to a scruffy expanse of untilled soil and an almost-empty barn, instead of boxing up their pots and pans and watching the last of their cattle being hauled away in the back of a truck.

"Your father abandoned us," Mom had said. And it came to Nate that he had.

"Don't drop it!" Junie called to Nate as he carried the cloud chamber wrapped in a blanket out to the car, in the rain, and set it in the back of the station wagon. Next to it was Uncle Harold's projector and the rolled-up poster drawings of the paths made by the different kinds of ionizing rays. On the other side he'd already loaded the cooler with the dry ice inside.

"I'm really proud of you, Nate," Mom told him, pulling out of the drive. "Whatever the judges say, you did a great job."

"The judges are going to love it," Junie said. "Wait till they see those sparkles start dancing all over the place."

They stopped by their grandparents' house to pick them up, then headed off to the school. In the gym the bleachers had been partially folded back toward the walls, and long rows of tables were set up to display the projects. When

Nate's family got there, the room was already filling up. Someone had built a guinea pig maze. Pots of beans, labeled with the names of different fertilizer combinations, were arranged in half a dozen different locations. Three kids had built model volcanoes, in which they would demonstrate eruptions. There was a girl with a jar full of cows' eyeballs that she planned to dissect—one per hour. Alongside it was a drawing of an oversized eyeball, side view, each part labeled with red arrows.

Nate found his spot—at a table along the back wall, directly underneath the basketball hoop. He set down the cloud chamber first and unwrapped it. Then he hung the poster, with the neat lettering his mother had penciled in for him to marker over: HOW RADIOACTIVE IONS TRAVEL THROUGH A CLOUD CHAMBER. BY NATHAN CHANCE AND NAOMI TORVALD. Next to the cloud chamber he put down first his cooler, then the bottle of ethyl alcohol, and finally, in the same velvet box it had come in back when Poppa had bought it in 1940, the watch. Nearby he positioned the projector so the light would hit the chamber just right, and he plugged it in using the extension cord he'd brought.

Nate was just dusting off the chamber's glass sides when a group of girls stopped at the table—Pauline Calhoun, her friend Jennifer, and a girl named Janice, who'd taken piano lessons from his mom when she was preparing for the county's Junior Miss pageant. She'd quit right after winning second runner-up.

"Great project, Nate," said Pauline, standing in front of Naomi's drawings of the alpha ray patterns. "I guess you must feel real bad about what happened to your partner, huh?"

Nate looked up from the table at her hard, pretty face. There was something about her eyes—a sharpness to the way they darted from his project to her friends—that made it uncomfortable to look at her.

"I miss Naomi," she said. "Don't you, Jennifer?"

Nate doubted that Pauline had ever spoken one word to his friend besides the mean ones that night at the bowling alley. He remembered them now—"I know you have my charm bracelet. Give it back." Most of all, he remembered the stunned look on Naomi's face when she told Pauline, "I never took anything. I don't steal."

"She was an interesting person," Pauline went on. It was odd, Nate thought, how people spoke about certain individuals as if they were dead, as if not being in their particular world anymore meant they didn't even exist.

"Naomi's fine," Nate said. "She and I did this project together. She just couldn't be here today."

Pauline and Jennifer exchanged looks.

"Hey, Pauline," Jennifer said in an oddly flat voice. "Did that bracelet of yours ever turn up?"

"No. But it sure was strange, the way it disappeared like

that." Pauline flicked her hair over her shoulder as the trio started to move on to the next display. "That night at the bowling alley, with nobody there but us and, you know, *them*."

After Nate had set everything up to his satisfaction, he and Junie left his table and circulated around the room. Once he would have felt funny to be seen at school with his little sister like this—even if she hadn't been wearing boots and a party dress with three different necklaces and a large rhinestone brooch of a horse. But today he held his sister's hand as they walked around the exhibits, and when she asked questions, he tried to come up with the answers.

Junie's favorite projects were those that featured animals, though she hated it when the experiment might have been bad for them, like the one in which someone's pet rabbit had been fed a diet of only soft food. The rabbit's teeth had grown so long, they curved out its mouth. She liked the guinea pig maze and "The Life Cycle of a Butterfly" and the project titled simply "My Cat," where Priscilla Ingersoll had just brought her cat to school, in a cat basket, with a report on his six and a half years of life to date.

Heading back to his display, Nate noticed his mother moving slowly through the room, examining the projects as the eyes of the other parents turned to follow her. She kept her hands wrapped tightly around her purse in a way Nate knew would keep them from trembling.

Her last stop was Nate's exhibit at the back of the gym. "I had no idea this would be such a big deal," she said when she reached him. "It looks wonderful. Your grandparents and I will be rooting for you from the bleachers."

Just as her mother left, Junie returned from up front, where she'd gone to check out the first-prize trophy. "It's not as big as I was picturing, but never mind," she whispered to Nate. "The really big ones are probably over in Butte."

Mrs. Unger stepped onto the stage. "People," she said, "I want to welcome you and thank you for attending the first annual Lonetree Junior High School Science Fair. As you can see, our youngsters have put a lot of time and effort into the projects displayed around the room. I know you're going to want to study each and every one."

Nate wasn't listening. He was worried about Amelia Swanson, who had built a pretty impressive display on electricity, with a series of batteries and wires hooked up to make three different-sounding buzzers go off depending on which button you pushed. Nate knew that Amelia's father was an electrician, but he doubted the judge did.

"Don't worry, Natie," Junie told him, following his eyes to Amelia's display. "Electricity's not that exciting. You've got genuine alpha rays."

•　　•　　•

While he waited for the judge to come by, Nate reviewed his file cards. The judge had already made one circuit around the room, but now he was stopping at each table, to give everyone a chance to talk about his or her project. Nate kept hoping Naomi would suddenly show up, in time to be there when he demonstrated the crackling sparks of radiation in their box.

"So what do we have here?" a man asked him. He was carrying a clipboard and wearing a large tag that said BOB FOLEY, JUDGE.

Nate began giving his report. As he did he tried to imagine he was his father, out in the barn when it was just the two of them—how he'd put it if he were explaining the cloud chamber to his son.

"You won't believe it," Junie said to the judge when Nate got to the part about the alpha rays. "Even if he wasn't my brother, I'd think he should get the prize."

"Interesting," the judge said. "Good job lettering the poster too."

"Our mom helped with that part," Junie put it. "But just wait till you see my brother's demonstration."

Wearing gloves, Nate took the dry ice out of the cooler, unwrapped it, and set the cloud chamber on top. He poured a capful of the alcohol onto the blotting paper. Everything was set. As Junie turned on the projector he took off his gloves and reached for the velvet box with the watch face inside.

"Junie," he said, "did you move the watch?"

"Of course not, silly."

They looked under the table, in Nate's book bag. The watch was nowhere.

"Just a second," Nate said to Bob Foley. "I can't find my radioactivity source. It's got to be here someplace."

Junie got down on her hands and knees and started checking the floor.

"I remember clearly setting it right next to my project," Nate told the judge. He was sweating now.

"I'm sure you did," the judge told Nate. "But I'd better be moving on to see the other youngsters' work. Very original choice of topic, though. Fine effort." He was writing something down on his clipboard. Then, incredibly, he was gone.

Nate was too stunned to move, but Junie pursued the judge. "You haven't seen what it does yet," she told Bob Foley at the next table. "It takes a minute or two to get the whole thing started. It can work even without my grandpa's watch."

"I'll have to take your word for it," said Mr. Foley. "I've got a lot of other work to judge."

"But the great part is the sparkles." Junie's voice had a pleading sound. "Even without the watch, there can be sparkles, from real stars."

Mr. Foley took a step back in Nate's direction, and for just a second Nate felt hope return. "The amazing thing is how they're around us all the time, every minute of the day. We just don't see them," Nate said. "In fact, most people have no idea."

Bob Foley looked up from his clipboard and straight at Nate's chest, as if something had finally caught his attention.

"Chance," he said, studying Nate's name tag. "You're from that family with the farm out on Bent Twig Road?"

"We have to sell it," Junie said. "There's going to be an auction."

"Right," Mr. Foley said. "I heard about that. My wife was thinking of checking it out."

Then he was gone, off looking at someone's fertilizer experiment.

A moment later it happened: A single spidery vein of light streaked through the cloud chamber like a shot from a ray gun.

The only problem was, nobody was there to see it but Junie and Nate.

For a moment Nate couldn't speak. Then he said, "Huh. Did you catch that, J? Our cloud chamber. It works after all."

"I knew it would," Junie said, but there was no joy in her voice.

At two o'clock Mrs. Unger and the school principal stepped on the stage to say the judge had chosen the winners. "But let's not forget," she said, "that every single one of you is a winner just for completing these fabulous projects and making so many discoveries about the wonderful world of science."

"Blah blah blah," Junie whispered.

Buddy Thick won an honorable mention for his project called "Why Cows Chew Their Cud." Third prize went to Jeannine Penney for her study, "Mr. Rogers's Ability to Calm Down Children." Second prize, Amelia Swanson, for "I Get a Charge out of Electricity."

The first-prize winner, who would be going on to the state finals all the way to Butte, was Violet Landry, for her project titled "How Relative Humidity Affects Making Fudge."

Mrs. Unger called Violet to the stage to receive her award and explain the project to the crowd.

"I chose this topic because I like candy and I particularly like eating fudge," Violet said. "Also, this is the time of the year when the weather varies a lot. I wanted to see which days would be best for making candy."

There was more, but Nate wasn't listening. He could feel the hot grasp of his sister's hand in his as they headed back to his table to pack up the cloud chamber. Somewhere in the room, he knew his mother and his grandparents were feeling bad for him. But all he could think of at the moment was Junie. He knelt down so he could look her in the eye. "I'm sorry," he said. "It was dumb to count on a stupid science fair to solve everything."

• • •

Poppa took the news about his lost watch better than Nate had expected. All he said was "Turns out I mostly know what time it is anyway." Walking out to the parking lot, he even put his arm over Nate's shoulder, something rare for him.

"Careful now," Poppa said as he lifted the back hatch of their mother's station wagon for Nate to set the cloud chamber inside. "That contraption looks breakable to me."

"So what if it breaks?" he said. "What difference would that make?"

Suddenly Nate could imagine how it had been for his father that day, standing out in the snow with his rifle cocked. He could imagine the moment when the pull of the black hole had gotten the best of him, and it seemed easier to let go. Nate thought about dropping the cloud chamber onto the blacktop—thought about taking off, right then and there, it didn't matter where. He had never needed more to see his dad, but even if he got to that hospital room in Warm Springs, what did he have to offer now, except the angry words exploding in his brain: *Don't you know, you messed up everything?*

Twenty-Eight

NATE HAD PICTURED THE AUCTION AS THE KIND OF event where five or six ranchers showed up, looked over his family's machinery, and offered a price. But the cars started pulling down their road just after seven, and by nine thirty there must have been thirty or forty vehicles parked in the field. People were milling around everywhere, wandering in and out of the barn, picking through the piles of their possessions.

Judd Payton, the auctioneer, had set up a tent with folding chairs in rows and a table at which a pair of women sat with an adding machine and a ledger book. They were giving out numbers to people for bidding. The auction wasn't due to start for another half hour, but already every seat was filled, and other people were standing around the piles of items up for sale.

Nate had known they were parting with the farm equipment, of course—the milker he'd spent so many hours operating, the old buckets he and his dad had hoisted all those years, the baler, the cider press, all his dad's tools.

What he hadn't pictured was the contents of their home spread out in the yard like that. There was the sofa he and Junie always sat on, watching their shows; the yellow Formica kitchen table where they ate; his mother's pots and pans; and his father's rocker, where his dad had spent the long, dark months from fall into winter, rocking back and forth, looking out the window to the snow-blanketed fields. There was his sister's old wagon that he used to pull her around in when she was little; Bucky's blue blanket; his mother's sewing machine. They weren't selling his mother's piano, but it had been set out on the porch for the movers to pick up the next day. A bunch of kids had gathered around it and were playing "Chopsticks." Someone must have opened the bench earlier and taken out his mother's sheet music. Now the pages were blowing over the field like old dry leaves.

Poppa had planted himself in the doorway to the barn, staring straight ahead like he was standing guard. Nate knew that he was feeling badly for not having been able to bail Nate's mother out from her debt to Sam Carter.

In the kitchen Grandma put an arm around Junie, who was quiet. "Your mother has things saved for you kids," she said. "She's got everything you need in boxes, don't you fret. Every one of those precious model horses of yours, honey."

The kitchen was bare—even the stove and the refriger- ator gone, with a white spot on the wall where the clock had been. His mother's typewriter still sat on the counter, and the empty gold box from the chocolates, which Junie had wanted to save—to hold her "special jewels." The living room was also bare, except for the TV and a couple of smaller chairs. They'd be taking those to Billings.

Upstairs Mom was vacuuming. She was in Junie's room now—also stripped, except for the bed and Junie's night table. A suitcase was open on the bed with Junie's clothes inside. It was pretty much the same in Nate's room, except for his baseball cards, his bat and glove, and a box of his books. "The movers will be over for the rest of our stuff tomorrow," his mom had told them. The beds. The dishes. The photograph album. The encyclopedias. Those had been his father's idea—bought from a traveling salesman who'd come by one afternoon when their mother was in town. She had burst into tears when she heard the price.

"How does a person place a value on knowledge, Helen?" he'd said. "Look at the name on the spine: World Book. These books will show our children the world."

Encyclopedias and binoculars, they had those. Just no home.

Outside, the auction had started, but Nate had chosen to stay in the house, away from the bidding. From where he sat at the top of the stairs, he watched Junie move through the rooms silently, touching the windowsills, stroking the counter, flushing the toilet in the bathroom, turning the water on and off. She opened a cupboard, closed it. Opened it again. "That's where we kept the Oreos," she said, as if she were visiting a museum.

He walked into his parents' bedroom. Only one dresser remained and his mother's little makeup table with the mirror attached, where Junie used to sit and play movie star. He was turning to go when a woman he didn't recognize stepped out of the closet.

"Oh," she said. "I thought there might be more stuff in here. Sorry." She hurried down the stairs.

There were marks on the wall next to the door, where his father had measured the two of them every January first; the spot on the rug where Junie had spilled India ink when she tried dying one of her horses black to look more like Pie in *National Velvet*. There was more, but he'd had enough.

Nate went back downstairs and out the door. He would've liked to go inside the barn one more time, but not with all the people there.

He walked out past the implement shed, away from the crowd and the crackling of the auctioneer's PA system, into which someone kept repeating "Testing, testing, testing." He stood on the spot where he and his father and sister had camped out to watch meteor showers. A girl was sitting in the grass, her hair a wild, frizzy corona around her head. Naomi.

"I got a ride from someone who was coming out," she said. "I thought you might need a friend."

"We didn't win the science fair," he told her. "We didn't even get a lousy honorable mention."

"I know," she said. "So that means no Butte. And no Warm Springs."

"Not for now, anyway. I'll figure something out."

"How's your little sister?"

"The way you'd think. How about you?"

"Same kind of deal," she said. "I just keep reminding myself that I am not going to let my parents ruin my life. Eventually, I get to make my own choices."

"I'll be going to a new school," Nate said.

They sat there for a couple of minutes, not saying anything.

"In the boys' room they wrote this stuff that said you were my girlfriend," he said finally.

"Probably the same type of junk they wrote in the girls' room. If it was me doing it, I would have made the drawings lots funnier."

"I just want you to know, I didn't cross it out," he said. "It wasn't like I thought that was so embarrassing."

"Even though we're not boyfriend-girlfriend," she added.

Naomi stood up. She did something surprising then. "I

thought I would kiss you," she said. "That way, in the future, if someone asks us, we can say we've done it before and we won't be lying. I figured it would save a lot of embarrassment."

She put her hands on his shoulders. She leaned slightly forward, close enough that her hair brushed against him. She closed her eyes and placed her mouth against his, very lightly. Then it was over.

"There," she said. "Now you can say you've got experience."

Their family had one last night at the house. After the auction Poppa and Grandma brought over sandwiches that they ate off paper plates on the floor, with a sheet laid out like they were having a picnic. Aunt Sal had asked, "Don't you think it would be better if Harold and I brought the children to our place tonight?" but Nate's mom had said no. She'd drop them off tomorrow on her way to Billings after the movers came.

"I promise you it's going to be better once we leave this place," Mom said when she tucked Junie in that night. Her voice sounded stronger than it had lately, and her hands weren't shaking. Then she went back downstairs, and Nate could hear her playing her piano on the dark porch and singing softly—the song he had loved when he was younger, "Over the Rainbow."

Sometime later Junie tiptoed into Nate's room and asked if she could climb into bed with him. "I promise I'll stay dry tonight," she said. "I'm over that now."

Lying in the dark next to Nate, Junie told him what it was that worried her the most. "What if our dad comes back to see us and we're not here? How will he ever find us?"

Twenty-Nine

SOMETIME IN THE MIDDLE OF THE NIGHT NATE WOKE up. He threw on a sweatshirt, grabbed his Polaroid camera, and made his way down the stairs. He wanted a picture of the cloud chamber.

Outside, it seemed that there had never been so many stars, but he didn't stop to study them. He was going to the implement shed. It was empty now, except for a handful of broken stuff and, on the old wood workbench, the cloud chamber.

There was a single chunk of dry ice left over, wrapped in newspaper, in the sawdust-covered cooler. He lifted it onto the workbench and placed the cloud chamber on top of it.

Slowly, like a mad scientist, he uncapped the ethyl alcohol and sprinkled it on the blotting paper. He replaced the top on the cloud chamber.

Poppa's watch was gone. If there were any rays to be

seen now, they'd be the kind that came from real stars, not a luminous-dial watch face.

He pointed the beam of the projector through the glass walls of the box and watched the gases begin to swirl and thicken. He stood there that way for a long time. There was one thing Nate had learned from years of milking cows and studying constellations—patience.

At first, when he saw the one dim flicker shooting through the box, he thought it was a dream. It felt like he was an astronaut floating up in space somewhere. His dad was there, and they were off on some intergalactic adventure. What he was seeing were the trails left by spaceships or meteor showers or an aurora borealis. Then he realized he was awake, and it was real, and he had managed to capture inside this box the sight he'd been waiting to see for so long. Here, in the middle-of-the-night darkness, was tangible evidence of a stellar explosion—the death of a star whose remnants had traveled millions of miles over millions of years to get to this implement shed in Montana, on the last night Nate would ever spend in the only home he'd ever known. And in all that time no living creature had ever seen what he was witnessing at this very moment. This particular spidery track of light, flashing for a nanosecond through the chamber, then moving on.

First it was only one, like at the science fair. Then another. Then suddenly the rays were shooting through the cloud chamber like atomic billiards, crashing and bouncing off one another, colliding and intersecting. It reminded Nate of that moment that Junie loved at the beginning of "Disney" every Sunday night, when Tinkerbell waved her wand and sprinkled fireworks across their television screen. Only this was much better.

He imagined how it would be if grief were something visible, like cosmic rays. He imagined what the airspace around their kitchen table would have looked like, these last months, if there had been a light to shine on it or some chemical compound to pour onto the linoleum that made it so they could see all the things they had been feeling.

Maybe, if they could have seen what was there, it would have resembled an animal—a monster—lurking in the corner. Not in the corner, even, but smack in the middle of the room. On the kitchen table, snoring loudly and giving off a terrible odor.

It came to Nate, standing in the darkness of the implement shed, that he and his sister had stared down two very different kinds of sorrow over this last, hard stretch of months. One was the sadness that came from having for your dad a man who didn't want to be alive anymore. The sadness of a rifle and a bullet and blood.

But there was another sorrow too. And that was what came after. The not talking. The pretending like things were no different. The loneliness of never getting to cry out to the people you loved best how angry and scared and broken-hearted you were. If his family could only have talked about what happened, they might have been able to comfort one another. The sorrow would have been there still, but it would have been so much better to shine the light on it.

Look, they could have said. *Here is what I feel. Over there is the monster I have to fight off. Over there is the mess he made when he came crashing in the room. There's the broom to clean it up. There's the space that was left, after.*

Angry as he'd been at his father lately, Nate knew what he wanted then. He wanted his dad to see this. Nobody would understand better the glory of this moment.

Nate lifted the Polaroid camera from the bench. There was a single picture sheet left. He put his eye to the viewfinder and snapped the picture button.

As he waited for the film to develop he ran through his pi digits. When he peeled back the paper, there it was, still damp: the image of a dark black box, its edges only barely visible. But inside the box—fuzzy yet unmistakable—you could clearly see a firestorm of cosmic rays from some long-ago-exploded star.

The last vestiges of the moon hung low over the horizon when Nate returned to the house, though dawn was approaching. In his room he leaned over his sister, sleeping in his bed, her horse Midnight pressed tight to her chest.

"Junie," he whispered. "You need to wake up now. You need to get dressed."

Her eyes opened, crusty with sleep. "I dreamed I had a horse named Poco," she said. "I dreamed I was riding on a cloud."

"We're going on a trip," he told her.

"It's still nighttime. Mom's not up yet."

"Mom's not coming with us. This is just our trip. To Warm Springs."

They dressed in the dark. Nate had a candy bar Naomi had given him and a pack of very old beef jerky he'd found under his bed when he cleaned out his room. "That's what's great about jerky," his father once told him. "It can't dry out because it starts out dry already. One thing that always comes in handy on an adventure is a stick of beef jerky."

They brushed their teeth in the kitchen. Nate made sure his sister went to the bathroom, the way his mother always told her to before a long trip. They were already out the door when she asked him, "How are we getting there?"

"In the car."

Nate had worried about what he'd do if he had to buy gas, but luckily, his mother had filled the tank the day before, which would give him enough, he hoped, to make it the three hundred miles to Warm Springs.

He opened the door on Junie's side, but he didn't slam

it shut in case the sound might wake their mother. "Buckle your seat belt, J," he told her. Then he went around to the driver's side and climbed in. As usual, their mom had left the key in the ignition.

"Are you allowed to drive?" she asked him. "Won't Mom be mad?"

"Probably." He turned the key. Slowly, he pulled out onto the gravel road.

"When will we get to see my dad?"

"Today."

"I wish I was wearing my cowboy boots."

"It doesn't matter, Junie. You look great just the way you are."

They were on the road now, heading toward town. They passed another station wagon delivering newspapers, and a milk truck. Nate sat as tall as he could in the seat, hands at ten and two, eyes on the road.

He had driven his dad's truck up to the mailboxes and back and plenty of times to the grain elevator. Then there'd been that time chasing Bucky. But he'd never driven more than a couple of miles before.

"Is it okay if I talk, or do you need your whole brain to concentrate?" Junie said after a while.

"You can talk," he told her, staring straight ahead. "Just don't ask me to do math problems or anything."

"I was just wondering," she said, "what you think it will

be like when we get to the place where Dad is. I was just wondering if it's a house or what."

"It's probably more like a hospital," Nate told her. "He might share his room with some other people, I don't know. He might even be in a bed."

"But he isn't really sick," she said. "He just got shot."

"He might not feel that good, Junie. He might be kind of sad."

"That's why we're going to see him, silly," she said. "To cheer him up."

They drove a long time. Now and then Nate checked their map, studying the names of towns: Harlowtown and Checkerboard and White Sulphur Springs. They passed Frenchie's, the restaurant where their grandparents took them once, and the turnoff for the county fairgrounds. Pretty soon there was nothing along the road but wheat fields and scrub. The prickly pear cactus was in bloom, and harebells and shooting stars, and with the windows open, Nate could breathe in the smell of sage, and the winter wheat was tall enough now that when the wind passed over, it made ripples, like a green and shimmering lake. The sun was just coming up, and Nate could see the silhouette of a fire lookout off in the distance and nothing else but sky beyond.

There were hardly any cars on the road, but when he

saw one coming toward them from the opposite direction, Nate could feel his whole body stiffen. He pulled the car over as far to the right as possible, almost onto the shoulder—worried that his mother must have reported him and his sister missing and that the police would be looking for them. But the car cruised on by.

"Hey, Junie," Nate said. "Do you mind scratching my ear? I don't want to take my hands off the steering wheel."

After a couple of hours, Junie needed to go to the bathroom. There were no rest stops on this stretch of road—no anything—so he pulled over, close to a little grove of alder by a creek. "You can go there, Junie," he told her. "Just use a leaf."

"Don't look."

"You nut. I've seen you in the tub a million times."

"I'm seven now."

Junie sang to him. "Yellow Submarine" and "Jimmy Crack Corn" and "The Twelve Days of Christmas," even though it wasn't exactly the season. She taught him a round from Brownies, "Make New Friends," and another one, "White Coral Bells." She told him about the platypus, one of the very few mammals that lay eggs, and how the pilgrims made cornmeal mush. She fell silent then, and for a while the only sound in the car was the hum of the engine and the wind.

They were climbing in elevation. The stretches of open land were behind them now, replaced by craggy boulders and outcroppings of rock. Off in the distance, they could see the foothills of the Rockies, with snow on top. Once or twice Nate spotted an elk, and he could feel a new chill in the air.

Although it was not even noon yet, clouds began to roll in and the wind started wailing. Nate turned on the heater and wished he'd brought their winter jackets. His fingers felt cold on the wheel, and Junie was shivering.

Then suddenly, like that scene in *The Wizard of Oz* where the tornado touches down, the sky grew dark. At first only a few snowflakes landed on the windshield, but within minutes, Nate and Junie were in the middle of a snowstorm. Nate turned the headlights and the windshield wipers on, but even so, he couldn't see more than a few feet in front of the car. The snowfall seemed to be coming at them sideways, like chaff from a thresher. Nate felt his stomach clench and his throat go dry. "I can't see where we're going, Junie," he told her. He was wondering if they should turn back.

"I know you can get us there," she said.

The road was winding steeper all the time, into the mountains. Nate passed a road sign that said CAUTION, FALLING ROCK and another indicating a place where trucks could pull off to the side if their brakes failed. On one side of them the rock face of the mountain rose like a giant tombstone. On the other, a total drop-off, with only rock and trees and boulders far below. As they climbed, every few twists in the road they'd come to a place where it would dip again, and Nate would feel the slippery surface under his tires. A couple of times he could feel the car losing traction, the beginnings of a skid. "Turn with it," his father had told him. "You'll want to put your foot on the brake when you start to slip, but don't let yourself do it."

He thought about his mother then, how worried she must be. She'd probably have called his grandpa by now, and Aunt Sal and Uncle Harold might be coming over in their pickup. Suddenly he felt tears come to his eyes, but he didn't want Junie to see.

"Let's hear a joke," he said.

"What did Humpty Dumpty say when he fell off the wall? . . . Ha-ha, you got yolk all over the place."

He knew this one. The punch line was supposed to be "The yolk's on you," but she'd gotten it messed up. "That's a good one," he told her, hands firmly gripping the steering wheel.

"Knock knock," Junie said soberly.

"Who's there?"

"The man from U.N.C.L.E."

"Huh?"

"It's the man from U.N.C.L.E., Natie," she said. "Wouldn't that be so funny, if that's who came over?"

"Yup, it sure would be," he said.

Then they were at the top of the mountain pass, the continental divide. On a clear day this would be an amazing spot to look out from. Now there was nothing but white. "We're going to be going down soon, Junie," he told her. "It'll start to get better."

"Natie," his sister said after the grade had become less steep and the snow had slowed down to gentle flurries. "There's something I need to tell you, but you might get mad."

"Okay. What?"

"You know when we were at the bowling alley with Naomi, and Pauline came over and said Naomi stole her bracelet? And everyone was thinking maybe she did?"

"Not me," Nate said.

"It wasn't Naomi that took the bracelet. It was me. I have it in my golden box."

Careful as he was to keep his eye on the road, Nate took a quick look at his sister. She was sitting very straight in her seat, and she was studying his face. Her horse was clasped in one hand, and her pocketbook, containing the new drawing of herself that she'd made for their father, was in the other. Her face registered a look of terrible uncertainty—as frightened as Nate's had been driving over the pass. He found a spot to pull over and turned off the car.

"I stole something one time," he said. "A few times,

actually. From a store. Baseball cards. I thought it would feel good to have them, but it didn't."

"I never even wore her dumb bracelet," Junie said. "I just kept it in my box."

"You know what we need to do, don't you?" he said, putting an arm around her. "You've got to give the bracelet back to Pauline, J. Even though we don't like her one bit, it's not okay to steal things like that."

"I know," she said. "And you've got to give back the cards."

"Just so you know," Nate said. "Pauline had it coming to her."

"Know what I think happened to Poppa's watch?" Junie said after a minute. "Know who I think took it? Back at the science fair, when we were walking around looking at other people's projects?"

"I think I do," he said.

The two of them spoke the answer at the same exact second: "*Pauline!*" Then they burst out laughing.

Even though she didn't mean to, Junie finally fell asleep, a little outside of Prairie City according to their map. By the time she woke up again, they were on the outskirts of Warm Springs. Off in the distance Nate could see a few tall buildings and grain elevators.

The fuel gauge was on empty. Nate had just enough gas

to pull over on the side of the road before the engine cut out altogether.

"Looks like we're walking the rest of the way, J," he told his sister, hopping out. She grabbed hold of his hand.

They walked along a street, with no idea where to go. A woman approached them, pushing a baby in a stroller.

"Excuse me," Junie said. "Do you know how to get to the mental hospital?" She said it firmly, like there was nothing to be ashamed about. "We're going to see my dad."

Thirty

THE HOSPITAL WAS AN OLD STONE BUILDING, THREE stories high, that looked like someplace the Addams Family might live. There was a rolling lawn out front, with benches scattered under the trees and a few people walking around.

Nate kept his eye out for a tall, thin figure of a man, but no one looked familiar.

"You sure you're ready?" he asked Junie when they'd climbed the hospital steps and he'd pushed open the door.

"Yes."

"You're a brave girl," Nate told her.

"And you're a great driver."

Inside there was a woman reading a book at a desk.

"We're here to see Carl Chance. I think he's a patient here."

The woman looked over the top of her glasses at the two of them. Until this moment Nate had not considered his sister's outfit. She was wearing the top to her *I Dream of*

Jeannie pajamas, printed to look like a harem outfit, her Brownie skirt, bright red tights, and Keds that used to be white. Around her neck, as usual, were a couple of her necklaces. Luckily, Nate was more conservatively dressed.

For a moment he imagined that the woman was reaching under the desk for some secret button that alerted security to the presence of unaccompanied children who had stolen a vehicle to come see their father. He pictured large men marching in from the recesses of the hallway—or women, in nurse uniforms, with hypodermic needles— ready to carry them away to some padded cell. *We've got a few more from that crazy Chance family,* one of them would say. *You know where to put them,* the head nurse would answer, and they'd exchange knowing glances. *The electric shock room.*

But the woman only flipped through the pages of her pad. "That would be the second floor. He might be in the sunroom right around now. You're with your mother, I suppose?"

"Yes," Nate said. Not even blinking. "She's in the ladies' room. We'll just go on ahead."

It was easy enough to locate the sunroom. All you had to do was follow the shaft of sunlight coming from the far end of the long corridor. As they passed the patients' rooms, they could hear sounds on the other side of the doors—yelling, once, and another time, whimpering. But the sunroom looked surprisingly cheerful, with tables set up, a couple of checkers games under way, two or three people entertaining visitors, and others watching television. *Andy Griffith* was on, not that Junie noticed. She had spotted their father.

He was sitting alone, in a chair by the window. Even from the back, they knew it was him.

He looked thinner than Nate remembered, and his hair had been cut very short, but he had the same proud forehead. Unlike some of the people here, whose chins almost rested on their chest, he sat upright, with his face to the window.

Junie reached him first. "Daddy!" she cried. She placed her hand on his sleeve. Then on his cheek.

He turned very slowly toward her. "June bug," he said. "Juniper girl."

"I came to visit," she said. "I brought Nate." She stood next to his chair, waiting, like the way she'd stood when their mother had brought her to a department store in town one time to visit Santa.

"Junie," he said again. Then, "Nathan." He was smiling, and his face looked more like his old self than Nate had expected. Still, there was something different too, and not just that he was thinner. His eyes, which had always looked so intently at everything, had a blankness to them, like the water of the catchment pond. Flat and still and nothing underneath the surface but mud. Then he tilted his head as if he were trying to pick up some kind of vibrations in the air. There was a questioning look, like he was trying to find them, even though they were right in front of him.

In his pocket Nate fingered the photograph he'd taken the night before. All the hours of his drive, he'd imagined how he'd show it to his father as he explained the cloud chamber. But suddenly a wave poured over him, like grain spilling into the silo, of grief and pity and regret. Studying his dad's face, he understood what nobody had told them all this time: His father was blind.

"I brought you a picture I made," Junie was telling him. "It's me on Bucky. I got to ride him!" She held the picture out. He didn't take it.

"You're going to have to describe your picture to me, Junie," he told her. "My eyes don't work anymore."

He stretched out his arms, and she climbed on his lap. She rubbed her face against his cheek. "Not too scratchy," she said. "You shaved."

"I must've known you were coming. I wanted to make a good impression."

Then she was crying. "I waited so long to see you. I kept wanting to see you, and they wouldn't let us. I kept thinking you were coming back, and you never did."

"I wanted to see you, too," he said.

All this time Nate just stood there, watching his father and his sister.

"Nate built a cloud chamber," Junie went on. "He was trying to win the science fair prize so we could come see you, but a girl got it instead, for a stupid project about making candy. Nate's was really the best."

"A cloud chamber," he said. "I always wanted to build one of those. Did you get to see the tracks the ions make?"

"Yes." Nate this time. His voice came out deep and low, almost like a man's.

"We had to give Bucky away," Junie told him. "I'm seven now. Nate got picked to be starting pitcher. I got a new pink bike and a model horse called Palomino Pal and another one that's named October Sky."

"How's your mother doing?" he asked. "I hope I didn't turn her hair gray."

"No, it's red," said Junie.

All those hours Nate had spent on the highway today . . . all those days and weeks before that he'd yearned to see his dad . . . and now here he was, standing right across from him, and he couldn't think of one thing to say.

"You know about the Beatles, right, Daddy?" Junie went on. "I'll sing you one of their best songs: *In the town where I was born,*" she began, her voice high and strong, "*lived a man who sailed to sea . . .*"

She sang the whole thing straight through, and their dad joined in on the chorus.

"Remember that time we made a campout?" she said. "Remember the shooting stars? Remember Ursa Major and Ursa Minor and Cygnus the swan and the Big Dipper?"

"How could I forget?" their father answered.

"Don't be sad," she said. "But we had to sell our house. We don't have any cows anymore. We sold your tractor, too."

"I wasn't a very good farmer," he told her.

"That's okay," she said. "Nobody's perfect. We're moving to Billings. But we had to come see you first, so you'd know how to find us."

"I'll be leaving this place soon," he told her. "I don't really need to stay here anymore."

"You're better now?" she asked.

Nate was afraid to ask the question that came next. Somehow his father seemed to know what Nate was thinking, though.

"I'm going to college," his father said. "I've been working things out so I can start in the fall, once I move into a rooming house over by the campus. I'm learning a way to read where you put your fingers on bumps on a page, called Braille, so I can study along with the other students."

"So all three of us will be going to school at the same time," Junie said. "I thought you knew everything already."

"Definitely not," he said. "I'm going to study physics. And lots of other things besides."

"We might not see you for a while after this," Junie told him. "I don't think our mom will let us."

"How did you get here, anyway?" he asked.

"Nate drove."

His father smiled. "Good for you, son. Don't make a habit of it just yet. But good for you."

"I love you so much, Daddy," Junie said as she climbed down off his lap.

"I couldn't love you one crumb more myself," he told her.

When his dad stood up, he actually seemed taller than Nate remembered.

He turned to face the two of them. Even though Nate hadn't said much of anything, his dad knew just where he was. He stood a little awkwardly, with his hands at his sides.

"I need to tell you something. I need to say this to you both, and I'd say it to your mother, too, if I could. I'm sorry. I'm just so sorry I did this to you all."

Junie hugged him then. "It's okay, Daddy," she said. "It doesn't matter. It's all okay now."

Nate couldn't say the same.

It *did* matter. It had changed everything, forever. His

heart was as sore as his legs would be if he'd run a hundred miles or climbed the tallest peak in the Rockies. He would never be the boy he'd been before. He would never forget what happened. The losses of the last few months stretched before him like a vast, nearly endless expanse of prairie, whose terrain would take him years to explore. An ocean, deeper than any diver could get to the bottom of. The sky.

"I forgive you, Dad," he said. Nate put his arms around him then. They stood that way long enough for Nate to feel the air come into his father's lungs and, very slowly, out again—feel the tight, stiff muscles of his body soften and relax. "You showed me so many things," Nate whispered.

It was getting dark outside. Inside the sunroom a man in a white uniform was carrying in trays.

"We need to talk about how we're going to get you home," their father said at last. "You were lucky on your drive over here, but I wouldn't want you driving back. Not to mention, everyone at home must be worried sick about you."

Nate studied his father's face then, more lined than before, but still his dad.

"Let's go call your mother," his father said, taking their hands and walking with them, very slowly, toward the hall-way, and the steps, the door, the lawn, and all the miles still to go.